The Parchment Scroll

Book Three

Highland Secrets Trilogy

THE PARCHMENT SCROLL

HIGHLAND SECRETS

BOOK THREE

by

C.A. SZAREK

Paper Dragon Publishing

The Parchment Scroll
C.A. Szarek

Highland Secrets Trilogy Book Three

Other Books by C.A. Szarek

<u>**Highland Secrets Trilogy & Companions—Historical Fantasy Romance**</u>

The Princess and The Laird (Highland Secrets Prequel)

The Tartan MP3 Player (Book One)

The Fae Ring (Book Two)

The Parchment Scroll (Book Three)

Highland Valentine (A Highland Secrets HEA Story)

Highlander's Portrait (A Highland Secrets Story)

<u>**Highland Treasures—Historical Fantasy Romance**</u>

Highland Oath (Book One)

Highland Essence (Book Two)

Highland Skies (Book Three)

<u>**The King's Riders—Fantasy Romance**</u>

Sword's Call (Book One)—*Also in Audio*

Love's Call (Book Two)—*Also in Audio*

Rogue's Call (Book Three)—*Also in Audio*

Fate's Call (A Novella from the World of the King's Riders) — *Also in Audio*

<u>**Crossing Forces — Romantic Suspense**</u>
Collision Force (Book One) — *Also in Audio*
Cole in Her Stocking (A Crossing Forces Christmas) — *FREE read!*
Chance Collision (Book Two) — *Also in Audio*
Calculated Collision (Book Three) — *Also in Audio*
Collision Control (Book Four) — *Also in Audio*
Weekend Collision (A Crossing Forces HEA Story) — *FREE read!*
Superior Collision (Book Five) — *Also in Audio*
Incendiary Collision (Book Six) — *Coming Soon!*

<u>**The Giovanni**</u>
King of Hearts (Book One) — *Also in Audio*
Queen of Diamonds (Book Two) — *Coming Soon!*

Dedication

This one is for Alison, Captain of the Word Count Police! Love ya, girl!

chapter one

"I'm not giving up. I have to find her." Jules listened to her partner drone on about needing her. He wanted her to come home to Texas. Now.

Too freaking bad.

"Jules, I hate that this happened, but what else can you do?" Dan asked.

She tried not to growl at him. "I'm a cop. I'm gonna do what I do."

"In another country?"

"Yes. You might as well leave off, Dan. I have two more weeks' vacation. Chief is cool with this. Why aren't you? Some support would be nice."

"I think you're setting yourself up for disappointment, is all. I'm worried about you."

"*Disappointment?* You're acting like this situation is over a missing puppy. We're talking about my baby sister. So, you can kiss my ass."

He sighed.

She pictured him shoving his hand through his dark hair like he always did when he was frustrated with her.

"I'm sorry, Jules. I'm not trying to be a dick, or

sound insensitive. It's just—"

"I know. It's been three weeks. If they're not found within the first forty-eight hours, they're usually not found. Or found alive. I am well aware." Jules didn't tell Dan about the scroll in her hand. Or that she'd seen—held—Claire in her arms on the beach.

She didn't believe a word on the parchment. Despite the fact it was written in her sister's neat, tight handwriting. "I know my sister. Something's not right. She didn't take off on her own."

Despite what the letter says.

Her partner sighed again, not answering right away. "Jules…"

"Look, I gotta go. I have an appointment with a guide, and I don't want to be late."

"Just be careful. Call me if you need anything."

"I will." Jules hung up the phone in the bright room of the hostel. She shook her head and glared at the broken MP3 player on the nightstand.

She'd hit every isle, every historic landmark, museum, even castle and quaint village Claire's tour group had traveled to.

No sign until Tuesday last week when her sister had fallen into her arms naked on the beach—literally appearing out of nowhere. Jules had hugged her and demanded to know where Claire's clothes were, as well as where she'd come from.

Hadn't gotten her anywhere.

If she didn't have the MP3 player and the piece of

parchment as proof, Jules might've thought she'd dreamed it.

Claire had told her to read the scroll. Said she'd gotten married.

Then she'd said she loved her, and... well, disappeared.

The rest was hazy.

Jules was still full of *what the hell?*

No logical explanation.

No sign of her sister, either.

Claire had told her she'd probably never see her again.

"Screw that." Jules made a fist but was careful not to crush the fragile scroll. She'd read the words more than a hundred times.

Still didn't believe them.

She sucked in a breath and sat hard on the bed. "What the hell am I supposed to do?" Jules closed her eyes and tugged at her messy ponytail.

Silence and a whole lotta *no answer* to her question.

Claire's all I have.

"Dammit," she muttered.

Jules stomped her feet into her boots and yanked the side zipper all the way up. She hadn't worn the clunky things since she was a patrol cop, but they came in handy trudging all over the rocky beaches of the Hebrides.

"Not that it's got me anywhere," she growled, yanking her backpack off the chair in the corner. She grabbed her hoodie and slipped it on. The weather was chilly, and warmer clothing was almost an afterthought, since Texas was usually pretty mild in the spring.

With a sigh, Jules slipped one of the bag's straps over her shoulder and surveyed the room. She had everything she needed to be gone all day, including two flashlights and food in her bag in case she got the munchies.

She didn't know the chick she was meeting at the pub. The woman was Irish—at least from her accent on the phone—and she'd called Jules in response to the missing persons ad she'd placed in the local paper.

What the caller knew about her sister was a mystery she'd refused to spill on the phone.

"Well, I'm about to find the hell out." Jules pulled her door shut.

"Goin' out?"

Jules plastered on a smile for the owner of the hostel when she made it to the foyer of the building. "Gonna check out that famous pub."

The older woman smiled. "Enjoy tha day."

She nodded, turning away without another word. The only way Jules would enjoy her day was if she found Claire.

The sea air made Jules close her eyes and take a deep breath. It permeated everything, but she didn't mind. The wind was clean and refreshing. Too bad she couldn't take a minute and enjoy the serenity.

Her sister had always been fascinated with Scotland, but until Jules had set foot on the Isle of Skye, she hadn't understood why. She could see the appeal now, with the sprawling green fields and rocky beaches, the castle ruins strewn about, and even buildings as much as eight or nine hundred years old still standing.

History and legend dominated the Hebrides and if she hadn't been on a mission, Jules would've loved exploring. Every place she'd visited had been beautiful, even if it was a bit cold.

Not to mention the accent—add it to a cute guy, and she could see why Claire would melt. She probably wouldn't get used to the tartan everywhere. It made Jules think of school uniforms.

Mostly male voices enveloped her as she opened the heavy wooden door into the place. The scent of musty wood and whiskey hit her senses, but the pub had charm. A sign boasted that it'd been established in 1792.

Jules waded through the mass of people, making her way to the bar, where she'd told the woman to meet her.

A good-looking redheaded man was wiping up a spill on the scarred dark-wood countertop as she slid onto a stool.

He flashed dimples when they made eye contact. "What can I get ya?" His accent was thick and appealed as much as the twinkle in his brown eyes.

"Just a water please."

"American?"

"Yes."

"Only water, lass?" He straightened and grabbed a glass from the stack on the counter behind him.

Lass. Another thing that would take some getting used to. Not like she was a spring chicken, at thirty-one.

Jules leaned into the edge of the bar and smiled at the guy anyway. "Yes, please. Too early for anything else."

He winked. "Not 'round here. Never too early fer a drink."

She laughed. Damn, he was charming. If she could take a minute to have fun, she wouldn't be opposed to asking him to show her around.

The bartender scooped ice into her glass and made a flourish of filling it from the tap.

Jules couldn't stop smiling, despite the weight that still settled over her chest. She sighed for the hundredth time that morning and sipped water, watching as the cute bartender moved on to fill another order. Every time she caught his eye he winked.

She glanced at her watch and frowned. Fidgeted on the stool. The chick that'd answered her ad was late. The caller had been the one to pick the pub, so she had to know where the place was.

I assume, anyway.

"What gives?" Jules dragged two fingers through the condensation clinging to the side of her glass.

Glancing over her shoulder, she scanned the pub, but no one seemed to be searching out someone they didn't know.

Small groups of mostly guys sat, chatting, or watching the television on the wall. Scottish brogues, as well as other accents — tourists like Jules — graced her ears, and the atmosphere made her shoulders loosen.

There was no urgency. People laughed as they talked, enjoying their food and drink. Two waitresses balanced trays as they moved around the place, both smiling as they interacted with patrons.

Jules swallowed sigh one hundred and one and studied the shelves of bottles perched on the wall across from her at the bar. All types of alcohol were on display, with the usual expensive stuff up top.

The words "By sea and by land" were carved into a wood plaque above the shelf. *MacDonald* was in all capital letters below it. Some sort of crest was beside that, wrapped in a plaid dominated by red. It was too dim in the bar to catch the rest of the colors.

The bartender shut the cash register drawer with a *ching* and threw her another wink. "Sure, I cannae get you somethin' else, lass?" He made his way to her. The smile he wore was infectious.

"No but thank you. Meeting someone."

"Ah. He shouldna keep you waitin'."

Jules grinned at the sudden disappointment on his face. "I'm just anxious 'cause *she's* late."

His broad shoulders loosened, that appealing

smile back in place.

Her eyes trailed his chest. The short-sleeved hunter green shirt wasn't skin-tight but hinted at defined pecs.

Jules tried not to stare or imagine his abs. It'd been a while since she'd been with anyone, and even longer since she'd had a relationship, and this guy was tall like she liked them.

Maybe she was just lonely.

"Rob MacDonald." He threw his hand out for a shake.

"Jules." She put her hand in his, liking the feel of his callused skin against her palm. "Nice to meet you."

"You, too. Jules, huh?" Her name in a Scottish accent made him even more tempting.

"Juliette, but it's too formal for me." She grinned.

"Jules fits you, like fine jewels."

If she was in her right mind, she'd roll her eyes and disregard the cheesy pick-up line, but she winked at Rob. "MacDonald, huh? Like that plaque up there?" She pointed.

"Aye. Clan MacDonald's crest. My family's been on Skye a long, long time."

So Jules had discovered when she'd looked into the history of the Isle of the Hebrides Claire had been most fascinated with. "MacDonald and MacLeod, right?"

Rob nodded. "Dunvegan, the MacLeod stronghold, still stands. Armadale, my clan's castle, dinnae, unfortunately. But there are ruins and gardens popular for weddins. Open for tours, I believe."

"I'll have to check that out."

His eyes grazed her face and Jules tried not to squirm.

Rob's lips parted as if he was going to say something.

Her gut screamed that he was going to volunteer to show her around.

"Juliette McGowan?" The feminine voice cut through the cute bartender's almost-proposition.

Dammit.

She would've said yes.

Jules swiveled the bar stool around. Her gaze collided with a pair of dark brown eyes. "That's me."

"I'm Bree. I can take ye to yer sister."

chapter two

Yup, the accent was Irish, not the distinctive Scottish brogue she'd grown used to since landing in the Highlands. The woman was dressed oddly, too. Red track pants sporting a white stripe from waist to ankle on the side, some tan hunting boots that looked three sizes too big, and a tight green V-neck shirt with purple and pink polka dots.

Bree was wearing a thrift store.

Or thrift store rejects.

Jules tried not to stare and slipped off the stool at the woman's urging.

"Come, let us find a more private place to speak."

She followed Bree to the back of the pub—in the darkest corner, really. Her pants *swoosh-swooshed* as she walked, and the boots *clunked.*

Definitely too big for her.

Bree slid into the booth, her eyes darting around the pub. She stared at the large flat screen TV mounted on the wall and swallowed. When she averted her eyes, she shifted on the padded seat, like she had some aversion to soccer—football as the UKers called it.

A cellphone rang and Bree jumped, a scowl twisting her mouth. She looked around again, rubbing her bare arm below her short sleeve, and fidgeted.

"Are you okay?" Jules asked as she took a seat across from her mystery caller.

Dark eyes darted to meet her gaze and Bree visibly shook. Then she squared her shoulders and sat taller. "I am well. Considerin'."

"Considering what?"

The woman shook her head, shifting her ebony hair. It was long and loose, hanging almost to her waist and swaying when they'd headed to their seats. No doubt it touched the bench's vinyl padding.

A waitress appeared at the edge of their table. "Can I get you lasses anythin'?" She smiled, flashing dimples. Her hair was red as well. She had to be the bartender's sister. The resemblance was clear.

Bree jumped again.

"No, I think we're good," Jules said.

"Call fer me if you change your minds. I'm Megan."

Jules nodded and turned back to her strange companion.

What's this chick's problem?

She was acting like she was tweaking on something — like meth.

If she was high on something, it wasn't meth, though. Her olive complexion was creamy and clear. Bree wore no makeup, and her face held no pockmarks, one of the physical side effects of frequent methamphetamine use.

If she's high, can I trust anything she's about to tell me?

"Ye look like her," Bree blurted.

"Where's my sister?" Jules demanded.

"No' where. *When.*"

Jules' heart kicked up a notch.

When.

Could Claire's scroll be true?

No.

"When?" she asked but stumbled over the one-word question.

"Aye."

They stared at each other in silence.

A cheer went up in a bar.

Jules didn't need to glance over her shoulder to know the Scottish team had scored. "How do you know my sister?" She forced the words out when the woman shifted on the bench, averting her eyes.

"I opened a portal ta this time by accident. She came through it, back ta *my* time." The words were even, understandable despite the thick Irish brogue.

It was Jules' turn to shift in the booth; her heart plummeted to her stomach. She schooled her expression, calling upon all the police professionalism she could muster.

It can't be true. Doesn't make sense.

"My grandma was Fae. So, I've magic." Bree's conversational tone—as if they were talking about the weather—made Jules swallow hard.

Her temples throbbed. "Magic?"

"Aye. The rift in time was an accident; I only meant to go into the Fae Realm."

Fae Realm?

Rift in time…

Jules couldn't muster words. She dug in her pocket. Her shaking hand slid the scroll across the table.

Bree accepted it; unrolled it but didn't look down long enough. "I cannae read. What does it say?"

"You can't read? Then how did you know to call me?"

"I saw Lady MacLeod's picture in the… the… newspaper, a man called it. I showed it to him. He dialed his… his… strange device. Yer voice came from it."

Jules smirked. "Cellphone? You're really not from around here, are you?"

Bree swallowed and shook her head. "Nay. I was born in the year of our Lord, sixteen hundred and forty-eight."

Jules gasped. "I don't believe this."

"What does the scroll say?" The woman looked back down at the words Claire had carefully inked onto the fragile parchment.

"It says that my sister went back in time, to 1672. It says that she's going to miss this guy, some Duncan MacLeod dude, and that she doesn't regret anything, but wanted him to know she loves him. That she didn't regret marrying him. It's written to *him*, but she gave it to me."

"Then ye know everythin'." Bree nodded and rolled the scroll tight. She reached across the table and put it in Jules' sweaty palm.

"Everything? I know *nothing*. This is all nonsense. Time travel? You've got to be kidding me."

"'Tis all true." Bree's voice was hard.

"All I know is that my sister disappeared four weeks ago. The damn tour company didn't bother to call me until days later. They didn't even call the police. *I* had to make the missing persons report. Then she appears on the beach and falls into my arms, *naked*. She gave me this," Jules pointed to the parchment, "then disappeared—literally."

"That's tha way of it. She went back."

"What?" Jules frowned. "You realize you sound crazy, right?"

Bree nodded. "I've no' been in yer time long," her voice cracked, "but I've learned magic is no longer revered. I cannae find anyone ta 'elp me get home." For the first time, the woman seemed to lose her cool. Her voice cracked, and her dark eyes were desperate.

"Revered? Because it's *not real*. That's why."

"'Tis real."

Jules sighed. "None of this is real. It has to be some dream. Some sick joke. I'll wake up in Texas. Claire will call me and complain about her job. I'll tell her to quit for the hundredth time, and we'll set up a lunch date, or plan to see a movie this weekend." She cursed the shake in her words and met the crazy chick's gaze.

Bree's eyes were misty. "I need ta get back ta my time." The words were fragmented; Jules could sense more desperation.

"Right."

When Jules met Bree's gaze again, she saw no more desperation—only determination. "Ye still dinnae believe? I'll show ye."

"This doesn't mean anything." Jules gestured to the weathered headstone. It was worn, but the etched words were still visible.

Claire MacLeod. Loving Wife to Duncan and devoted mother to her children.

Right above the eighteenth-century date that didn't make any sense in relation to her sister.

"And we'd better go. I think we're on private property or something." Jules' words were rushed, and she swallowed hard.

Bree arched a dark eyebrow but said nothing.

"I mean, Claire is an English name. It was common even then, wasn't it?" Jules drummed her fingertips on her bottom lip, her heart thundering.

"'Lovin' wife a' Duncan?'" Bree's whisper went ignored as she started to pace.

"It means nothing. Duncan's a common Scottish name. I'm sure there was some other Duncan MacLeod.

Some other chick named Claire."

"This is tha proof ye demanded, since a letter written by yer sister's own hand isnae enough."

Jules stared at the boots she was forcing in the damp grass around her sister's— "*No*. Just, no freaking way." She made a cutting gesture with her hand.

"Nay? There isnae a date of birth. Dinnae that mean somethin' ta ye?"

Jules stilled, meeting her companion's deep brown eyes. "None of this means anything to me. Except that Claire is still missing."

"She's no' missin'."

"She is."

Bree crossed her arms over her chest. "I've more I can show ye."

"Like what?"

Why did you say that, idiot?

You don't need to feed into her shit.

The chick would see it as a dare.

"There's no middle name," she blurted before Bree could speak. "Claire's middle name is Grace. It doesn't say that on there."

"Dinnae matter." Bree's voice was hard, as was her expression.

"It *does* matter." Jules sucked in a very un-cop-like whimper.

It just can't be.

Repeating it over and over did nothing to change the scroll in her pocket, the headstone on the ground in front of her, and the Irish woman claiming to be from 1672 beside her.

"Ye *still* dinnae believe?"

Jules shook her head because a bodily response was all she could manage. Easier than words.

"Verra well. I shall take ye to the Faery Stones."

"Faery Stones?"

Bree nodded. "The portal is opened through the magic of the Faery Stones."

"If you have that all figured out, why are you still here? Why don't you just go home? What's the catch?"

Pink kissed the Irish woman's high cheek bones. "I cannae do it myself."

"Why?"

"Magic is weak in the Realm of the Humans."

"Realm of the Humans?" Jules frowned.

"Aye. Only when I was in the Realm of the Fae did my magic come easily for me."

"Realm of the Fae?"

Wait. She said that at the pub, too.

"Lady, just when I think I can start to make sense of things, you take it another turn for nutso." She might have laughed in another situation. Or helped Bree find a psych ward.

"I'm no' a lady." Bree sighed and cast her eyes upward. "I know no' wha' ta do to have ye believe wha' is right before yer eyes."

"Nothing. None of this is real. But for you, and what you've got going on here," she gestured to Bree's mismatched outfit. "Well, they have meds for that."

Dark brow knotted; Bree stared.

Is she insulted, or is that confusion for real?

"Perhaps I've made a mistake seekin' ye ou'."

"Look, I just want to find my sister."

"I've tol' ye I can take ye to her. Ye've but to believe."

"Believe? What does my belief or disbelief have to do with *anything*?"

"Everythin'. If ye dinnae believe, ye cannae help me."

"Help you? I thought *you* were supposed to be helping *me*."

Bree sighed as if Jules should've known exactly what she was talking about. Maybe she would've if they *both* lived in Looneyville.

"I cannae open the Faery Stones without yer help."

"What?"

chapter three

Jules couldn't quit shaking her head, even as they trudged away from their little illegal trespassing venture to the private Clan MacLeod cemetery. "What now?" She jogged to catch up to Bree, who was walking faster despite the too-big boots.

"I need ta go home."

"Why so urgent? Can't hack the twenty-first century?" Jules smirked.

Bree paused to throw a glare at her. "I dinnae belong here."

"Claire—if any of this crap is true—doesn't belong in 1672, either."

"She does now. She found love. Wed the laird." Her voice broke, and those dark eyes clouded.

Jules' gut said Bree lost someone close to her, but if so, why was she in such a hurry to get back? Wouldn't it make more sense to run from the pain?

Then again, there's a huge difference in our times, even the basic stuff. I mean if she's not lying. Or crazy.

The woman opened and closed her fists, holding them tight to her sides. Grief flipped to anger and slid across Bree's face, but she schooled her expression so fast, Jules could've been seeing things, even if her police instincts noted it.

"You okay?"

A nod was all the response she got, then Bree clunked through the ground cover, until fields bled into sand and rock. They were headed toward the beach.

Jules could hear the waves crashing, and crisp sea air teased her nose. "It really is beautiful here," she whispered.

"I prefer the Emerald Isle, meself."

"Of course, we're always partial to our homeland."

Again, Bree nodded, and silence fell, except for the *swoosh-swoosh* of her pants, and their collective boots crunching pebbles.

"Where are we going?" Jules asked after they'd jumped down an incline and hit deeper sand. Wind blew her hair in her face, and she tossed her ponytail over her shoulder. Wisps of hair that'd escaped tickled her forehead, but she ignored the urge to shove them away.

"The Faery Stones."

She didn't know what to say to that. Didn't matter that Bree had explained what the supposed portal was.

God, I've lost it.

On the other hand, had she really?

It wasn't like she believed any of Bree's crap.

Then why are you following her like a lost puppy?

Hanging on her every word?

"I'm not hanging on her every word," Jules

whispered.

"Pardon?" Bree glanced over her shoulder.

"Nothing."

A dark eyebrow arched, but soon she was discarded, and the Irish woman traipsed on.

"How am I supposed to help you, anyway?" Jules asked.

"I cannae open the Faery Stones withou' ye."

"Pardon?" she plucked out the word Bree had used earlier.

No answer.

Irritation rose from her gut as she followed Bree. However, her desperation was equal, so what could Jules really do?

She didn't believe any of this stuff, so what harm could come from sticking around just a little while longer?

They walked down the beach until Jules' calves burned from exertion. She bit back the *'are we there yet?'* playing on the tip of her tongue.

When Bree finally stopped, it was too quick, and Jules almost plowed the shorter woman over. "Geez, maybe you should warn a chick," she muttered.

The woman threw her an apologetic look. "Sorry, when I leave fer a while, I always have ta seek the Stones out again. Somethin' of the protection spell must remain. The location is hazy until I am standin' a 'fore it."

Jules didn't answer as Bree slid forward toward a

crack in the cliff side in front of them. The Irish chick felt around, both palms to the rock.

A gull screeched overhead, and Jules glanced over her shoulder to watch it swoop down to the choppy water. Another bird answered the call and joined the fishing expedition. She jumped when Bree called her name.

Bree gestured.

Jules forced one combat boot in front of the other to answer the woman's beck and call, chiding herself at the same time. "Where are we going?"

Irritation flashed in that dark gaze. "The Faery Stones, as I've told ye."

"Where exactly are they?"

"Inside. Come forth." As she spoke, Bree inched into the crack in the cliff wall. She turned sideways, but there was some clearance in front of her body.

"Inside?"

"'Tis a cave." Her words echoed as she moved forward.

"A cave. What about…animals? I'm not going in there." Jules groaned. Whining wasn't her style.

Woman up, and get this shit done.

Maybe I can check Bree into the psych ward when we're done and manage to not fill the bed next to hers.

She slipped her backpack off. Wouldn't fit through the narrow opening wearing it. Jules unzipped the small pocket in the front, grabbing her flashlight and grumbling as she followed.

"'Tis safe," Bree called. Her voice sounded deeper, but clear.

She said nothing more, but Jules could hear the scrape of her boots on the ground.

Water dripped from somewhere in front of them, echoing as Jules entered darker territory. She let the beam of her light lead the way, and the path opened up after a few feet. Air fluffed the wisps of hair around her face, so there was probably a crack or entrance on the other side, though she couldn't see much, including Bree.

The further she went, the more space she had to move around. The place was sizable, with a humid warmth that made her skin prickle, but the air smelled clean, not dank.

"Bree?"

"Here."

Jules zoned in on the voice.

Bree was flitting around the cave, lighting candles. "The cave looks different in my time, but it's as large as then. The entrance has changed. Was much wider."

"It's been a long time, probably erosion."

"Erosion?" The Irish woman paused, holding one candle above the other. They looked as if they were modern-day stick-candles found at any department store, but Jules didn't ask how Bree had gotten them.

"Natural wearing, from weather and stuff." Jules looked around as her eyes adjusted to the dimness, scanning the open space.

For a cave, it looked lived-in.

"I dinnae have much, but—"

"You've been living here? Sleeping here?" Jules frowned. Blankets were piled in one corner of the cavern.

"Aye. I've nowhere else ta go." Bree's voice shook. Nervous, in a way that belied the confidence she'd displayed since they'd met.

Jules *almost* felt bad for her. "So where are these Stones you've been talking about all day?"

"There." Bree gestured to the right.

"Geez, how did I miss them?" she whispered, inspecting the odd sight before her.

Five stalagmites rose from the cave-floor, one in the center of a semi-circle of the other four, and a few inches taller than the rest. That wasn't the weird part— after all, they *were* in a cave.

The semi-circle was perfect, as if it had been placed there, not grown. Each of the natural pillars had a large crystal on top of it. Actually, the crystal *was* the top of the stalagmite, as if the formation had melded into a crystal as it'd grown.

"Weird."

"Faery Stones." Bree's voice held reverence. Her chest rose and fell as if she panted, and her hands opened and closed at her sides.

"You okay?"

"Aye." She fidgeted in her too-big clunky boots.

"You sure?"

Bree nodded. "I will get home, with yer help."

"And I'll get my sister with yours."

"Aye." The Irish woman smiled. She really was a pretty girl. Too bad the wild look in her eyes offset it. Screamed *crazy*.

"There you go again, cuckoo for Cocoa Puffs just when I think you could be normal."

Shoulders tight, Bree cocked her head to one side. "What?"

"Never mind. What's the next step?"

"I am goin' ta open the Stones." Bree darted forward, whispering something Jules didn't catch. She caressed the crystal in the middle, then tapped the others in what had to be some pattern. The woman crooned to each one.

Jules rolled her eyes.

Really, this chick is nuts.

"I need ye ta come here," Bree said after several minutes of repeating her actions with no result Jules could see.

"Oh yeah? What for?"

The woman frowned but said nothing.

Jules sighed and approached the stalagmites. She buried her hand in her jeans' pocket, squeezing the small scroll when she found it.

"Touch tha crystal in the middle, then the others, right ta left one after 'nother."

She did as she was told.

Nothing.

Bree made a noise deep in her throat. "It *has* ta work this time."

Jules didn't answer but saw frustration in her companion's eyes when their gazes met.

"Let us try together," Bree declared.

Shrugging, Jules followed Bree's lead when the woman touched the Stones in order again, one of her hands on each Stone when Jules' fingers rested there at the same time.

Humming startled her. It too, was a pattern, one echoing the other in order. "Oh my God, is that *from* the crystals?"

"Aye. Do it again." Bree's words were rushed. Beads of sweat bathed her forehead.

Jules didn't argue, nor did she fight the Irish woman when Bree took one of her hands in hers, moving in the pattern and chanting louder.

Wind kicked up from nowhere, knocking Jules' backpack over with a *thump*.

Bree had her hand, so she couldn't grab it if she wanted to.

"What's happening?" She had to raise her voice to be heard over the moving air.

"It's workin'!" Bree had to shout, too.

The crystal beneath their joined hands lit up. Jules squinted against the radiance. Moving air whipped her ponytail in her face.

"Put yer other hand on tha' one," Bree ordered without looking up. She was chanting again under her breath.

Jules swallowed and clutched the small scroll to her sweaty palm. She should put it back in her pocket but didn't want to take the time. She commanded her shaking hand to the crystal to her right.

Finally, her fingers made purchase, the parchment stuck between her palm and the bright mineral. At her touch, it shone like she'd hit some *on* switch.

Bree's chanting became yelling.

The crystals were humming together now and heating up, like they were water on the stove, on the way to a slow boil.

A shudder made its way down Jules' spine, but she forced her concentration on the Irish woman, battling revulsion against the fascination that was creeping up from her gut.

Was she seeing magic?

Real magic?

"What e'er ye do, dinnae let go!" Bree's shout brought Jules' gaze to hers.

She gasped.

Bree was radiant, glowing like the five crystals. Her hair was flowing around her face, and her pants sounded like a parachute as the wind buffeted them.

"Willna be long now!"

Jules didn't get a chance to ask what she'd meant. Cool air smacked her face and dried her eyes. She had to squint.

There was a *pop*, then another, each getting

steadily louder until her ears rang. Light shot straight up from the crystal in the middle.

A triumphant whoop sounded from Bree.

Jules couldn't tear her eyes away as a bubble formed and hovered over the rocky ground of the cavern. It was hazy, widening slowly, getting larger and larger. It moved up and down as it grew.

"Home; I'm goin' home." The words were Bree's mantra, said over and over until the Irish woman switched to the other language again.

Disbelief whipped through Jules' form, as sure as the wind still pushing at her body and tearing at her clothing. She shook from head to toe.

"Come, come, it shan't stay open long." Bree gestured. "Ye can let go now."

Forcing a nod, she pried her fingers from the hot crystals, clutching the scroll tight. She had to lock her knees so she wouldn't fall over.

"Ye believe, after all." Satisfaction soaked the woman's statement, but she only smirked when Jules shook her head. Bree slid her arm in Jules' and tugged her forward, to the hazy bubble. "Let us go home."

Jules gulped but didn't pull away.

Just what am I getting myself into?

chapter four

ugh grunted as Dubh shot down the beach. He gave his great stallion free rein, the wind parting his hair and Dubh's mane alike. When the horse slowed of his own accord, Hugh closed his eyes and sucked in fresh, frigid sea air. He weaved his fingers in his horse's thick black mane.

The stallion snorted and slowed to a walk. His ears pitched forward and he hooved the rocky sand.

"Wha' 'tis it, laddie?" He patted Dubh's neck and looked around.

They were close to MacLeod lands. Needed to move back down the beach.

A feminine moan had Hugh freezing on his horse's back.

A lass?

The female in question was up ahead, wobbling on her feet not far from the rocky hillside. She had her hand at her forehead.

Also…she was naked.

Too much drink?

Hugh kneed Dubh, navigating the slight incline. When the stallion trotted within a few feet of the lass, he reined him in, slipping off his back. He patted his rump as soon as his deerskin boots hit the ground, but the horse wouldn't go far. Even if Dubh wandered, he'd return to Hugh's side with a whistle alone.

Frowning, Hugh watched the lass stumble. As if she was aware of nothing. Her arm shot out to steady her body but found no purchase.

What a body it was.

The lass had large high breasts, a slim waist, and hips that had just the right amount of curve. His eyes rested at the apex of her thighs. Barely-there honey-colored curls guarded the heaven between her legs.

He should feel a touch of guilt for looking at a stranger's intimate places, but he couldn't. Or he just didn't.

She whimpered and lurched toward him, but Hugh couldn't be sure she even realized she was no longer alone.

He took two steps forward, but she lost her balance before he could grab her.

The lass collapsed at his feet.

Something small and cylindrical rolled away and Hugh stopped it with a boot before the wind could send it flying. He glanced at the lass, but she was very still.

She'd passed out.

He bent and snatched up what he recognized as a piece of rolled parchment, paying it little notice as he buried it in his trews' pocket.

Hugh adjusted his sword so the scabbard

wouldn't poke him and squatted next to the lass.

She'd landed on her side, one arm above her head, and the other across her belly. His gaze trailed her shapely form once again. One of her legs was over the other, blocking her sex. Preventing him from closer inspection of the dark-blonde curls he'd seen.

His eyes landed on her breasts. They were as plump and perfect as he'd already observed. Her nipples were peaked, probably because of the chill in the air.

Perhaps he should look away, but no one had ever accused him of being chivalrous—and after all, he *was* a man. His cock certainly liked his perusal of the female foundling.

If he truly was the barbarian, they'd all assumed, he'd be doing a lot more than *looking* at a beautiful naked lass.

Hugh snorted and pushed rich golden locks out of her face. Her lashes were long against her high cheekbones. Her hair was wavy, settling over her shoulders and against her back. He stopped himself from stroking her cheek. His gut told him it would be silky and leave him with the drive for more.

He frowned. The urge to part her thighs and slip inside her was one thing, but to caress her with a gentle hand?

That hadn't been his way even with—

Hugh shook his head, growling.

He never thought about *her*, let alone said her

name in his head, and today was *not* the day to change his ways.

The lass on the loamy ground stirred, blinking up at him, but her green eyes were cloudy.

"Lass?" Hugh ventured.

Her brow knitted, and she moved her head back for forth, trying to look around. A groan fell from her lips, and her lush mouth parted. Her breasts rose and fell as she sucked in breath, and she rolled onto her back, blinking a few more times. She now lay spread before him, on display as if he'd wished it.

Hugh had to swallow hard. "Lass, can ye stand?" His words were rushed and cracked, but he needed her on her feet—and covered up.

She still said nothing as he grabbed her hands, but the lass didn't fight him as he hauled her to her feet.

Perhaps she's a mute?

As soon as he was sure she wouldn't tumble to the beach, Hugh took a step back and whipped his tunic over his head.

He had to lift her arms like a bairn to get her into his shirt. Even though she was a tall lass, it was huge on her, falling almost to her knees.

Hugh tilted her face up, forcing her to meet his eyes.

Hers were leaf green, as bonnie as she.

She blinked and swallowed, making him want to kiss her throat.

Hugh chided himself for yet another odd desire.

"Lass? Are ye wit' me?"

The lass jumped in his grip but didn't pull away. Her eyes darted left, then right, before looking back up at him. She muttered something nonsensical, then her hands curled around his wrists, but she didn't pull away from his fingers still cupping her cheeks.

Her pink tongue slipped out, running along her bottom lip and Hugh's mouth went dry.

When their gazes collided, he couldn't help himself. He dipped his head down and took her mouth.

Soft.

Her lips were soft and sweet.

He forced her mouth open and invaded, pushing his tongue deep. Hugh nibbled at her lips, urging her to return his kiss, tightening his grip on her face.

His manhood twitched, and he wanted to draw her into his arms, deepen the kiss and hold her close. Run his hands over her perfect backside, touch her hips, and bury his hand—then his cock—between her legs.

Hugh slanted his mouth over hers again, trying to coax a response.

Her tongue tentatively touched his, rubbing, moving slowly, kissing back gently.

Right as the triumph of getting her to return his gesture started to wash over him, the lass yelped and shoved him away with both palms flat to his bare chest. She ripped her mouth from his before Hugh had time to react.

Her eyes went wide when their gazes met, but her mouth was still open, and he wanted to taste her again.

"What are you doing?" she demanded, but Hugh didn't miss her flushed cheeks or how her breasts heaved. Too bad they were now hidden by his own garment.

"The lass speaks." He cleared his throat.

"Who are you?" Honey colored hair flew around her face as she backed up, frantically looking around the beach.

Hugh stared. Her inflection was odd. Like nothing he'd ever heard, but he could make out her words—and her anger.

Her emerald eyes shot daggers at him as she regained her composure. She could be angry all she wanted; Hugh wasn't about to apologize for the kiss he'd stolen.

The lass was sweet.

He wanted more.

Besides, he was a barbarian, was he not?

She startled when she looked down and noticed what she was wearing. Froze where she stood. Some unnamed emotion darted across her beautiful face, but she put her fingertips to her lips.

He wanted to tell her it pleased him, and ask if she could still taste him there, but nothing would come out of his mouth.

"Naked," the lass whispered. She looked around again, and Hugh could feel her desperation.

He frowned. "Aye."

Hugh took a step toward her, but she slid back, inching closer to the water.

"I-I-I— "

"Lass," he said.

"I never believed." The words had a frantic edge, and she swallowed hard—twice.

"Believed what?"

Her eyes were even wider when she met his gaze again. "Where's Bree?" She looked around, then shook her head when she didn't see whoever *Bree* was. Her gaze darted down to the sand around their feet. "Where's my scroll? Oh, God. I need it. Claire." She rushed away from him, looking down as she went.

"Lass," Hugh called, but she didn't respond. He growled to himself, and shot forward, his hand swallowing her upper arm.

She stilled, but he didn't miss the glare when she glanced up at him. "Let me go."

He pulled the small piece of parchment from his trews. "Is this wha' ye seek?"

The lass made a go for the scroll, but Hugh raised it above her reach.

"Give it to me," she ordered, anger darting across that pretty face.

Hugh chuckled when she jumped but failed to reach. "Jus' what do we have here?"

"None of your business."

He ignored his foundling and unrolled the

parchment. The lass's arms shot around his waist in the effort to tug him back to her, but Hugh grabbed her wrist and she whimpered. He held the scroll high, but where he could read it, and scanned the thing.

Her breasts against his back were a distraction, but he tried to ignore the soft press and focused on the neatly written words before him.

Hugh scowled at the first mention of *MacLeod.* Then '*marrying you,*' caught his attention. He'd heard that fool Duncan had found himself a wife, but it had been over two years ago now…actually, almost three. He read on, seeing some nonsense about the Fae, magic, and…traveling through time? "Claire," he whispered.

The lass froze in his grip.

He hauled his foundling around to the front of his body, pinning her to his chest. Hugh liked the feel of her in his arms.

Uncertainty flashed in those green eyes when their gazes met, and she struggled.

Hugh tightened his grip but tried not to hurt her. "Are ye Claire?"

"No."

Hugh arched an eyebrow. "Then have I found myself a thief?"

The lass frowned. "No."

He studied her face, resisting the urge to take her mouth again. Hugh saw no dishonesty in her steady gaze. The hesitation he'd read just moments before was now determination.

Her green eyes glinted.

A dare.

This lass is strong.

Hugh smiled slowly.

She glared up at him, her tempting lips set in a hard line. "Let me go."

"Nay."

The lass's eyes threatened to slay him on the spot. She bent her knee and made a jab for his tender parts.

Twisting his hips was the only thing that saved him.

His move adjusted her aim, but her shot ended up in his thigh, pain lanced down his leg.

Hugh barely maintained his hold. "Why'd ye do tha'?" he growled.

"I warned you." Her words dripped her ire, and she tugged against his hold. "What are you, some kind of barbarian? Let me go!"

He held on. There was no way he was going to release her now. The shifting of his grip hiked his tunic up, baring the creamy skin of her upper thigh.

Hugh tried not to stare there, or worse, rip the scrap of linen off her and show her what *barbarian* meant. "Well, lass, I dinnae ken who ye are, but yer likely important ta Duncan MacLeod, so yer comin' with me."

"What?" she screeched when he swung her up over his shoulder.

Hugh smacked her delectable rear end; couldn't help himself.   He chuckled when she yelped and pinned her legs to his chest when she started kicking him.

"Put me down!" Her fists pounded his bare back.

He laughed and whistled for Dubh.

CHAPTER FIVE

Jules struggled to no avail. The man's hands were like iron on her waist, and she was laid across the back of a huge black horse, so if she fought him harder, she would probably fall off and hit her head. "Let me go!" she commanded for the billionth time.

Air hit her bare ass, and she couldn't even reach to yank the shirt down over it. He had her face-down, arms pinned, and damn horseflesh cut into her stomach, stealing her breath. Blood rushed to her head, making her pulse pound in her temples. Jules wiggled, but he held her tighter. "Seriously! Let. Me. Go."

He chuckled and held on with only *one* of his hands.

God, he's strong.

The guy was *huge*, too. She was tall for a girl, at five-ten, but this dude had towered over her on the beach. He had to be six-five or six-six, and he was broad, well-muscled, like he lived in the gym. He was hot, too, which just pissed her off. His long dark hair kissed his shoulders, and he had eyes to match.

Another breeze ruffled the shirt, shooting air up her spine. She clenched her thighs and whimpered. No doubt he could see her *everything*.

His grip burned through the thin linen of the tunic, but he wasn't hurting her.

Not really.

"Hope you're enjoying the view," Jules bit at him.

A deep chuckle teased her ears—and made her gut roil.

She kicked her legs, trying to flip over and hit him. She'd always *hated* being restrained, even back in police academy days.

"Calm yerself lass, or ye'll fall off my horse."

Jules froze when she felt his big hands on her bare thighs.

He brushed higher, getting closer to her girly parts, so she yanked her arm from beneath her and tried to punch his side.

The guy released the hold on her thighs—he only had two hands, after all—and she was able to get a hit in as he tried to grab her wrists.

He missed, she rolled, and clocked him in the 'nads. Dude cursed—she guessed, it wasn't English—and Jules took the opportunity to slip from the horse's back.

She landed so hard her bare feet shot pain all the way up to her knees, but the best part was the shock on his face.

Her captor had one hand on his crotch, and those dark eyes were wide. His Adam's apple bobbed as he swallowed, staring at her.

"Later, sucker!"

Jules ran. Harder than she'd ever had to go after a suspect. Her lungs burned, her legs seared all the way into her quads, and her feet were on fire. Maybe bleeding from the rocky terrain, but she didn't stop to inspect them.

Hooves on her heels made her push harder.

He was yelling curses and orders from best she could tell, but Jules kept going even after she heard the *thud* of boots hitting the ground.

She didn't look over her shoulder to see where he was, but he was taller and had a longer stride than her, so she didn't have a chance if she hesitated even for a second.

Hard hands seized her from behind, and then she was enveloped in his heat. He lifted her off the ground effortlessly and said nothing.

The guy stalked to the horse and threw her on its back, but this time he sat her up properly, swinging up behind her before she had time to react, or think about her bare ass on horsehair—there was no saddle. He wrapped her in his arms and lifted her so she was sitting on his lap, then pinned her to him. The sound he made deep in his throat shot awareness down her spine and Jules squirmed.

She could feel his anger.

He was seething, but he still hadn't hurt her, despite the steel hold he had going on. His bare chest was hot against her back.

What a chest it was.

Despite her own anger, her body was aware of every hard muscle, every defined line she could feel through the shirt she was wearing.

His shirt.

Jules tingled all over, against her will, worse than when he'd kissed her. She shivered and it had nothing to do with the chilly air. After all, she was still flushed from her escape attempt.

What the hell was that kiss about, anyway?

Ugh, don't even think about it.

"Where'd ye think ye were goin'?" the man barked finally.

"Away from you."

He growled again, squeezing his arms around her. His hand brushed her belly, then inched up, as if he was contemplating going higher.

"Stop it." Jules jolted in his arms.

He laughed.

Asshole.

Fury burned and she dug her nails into his wrists. "Are you in the habit of kissing strangers and kidnapping them?"

"Are *ye* in the habit of wandering naked on the beach?"

Naked.

Like Claire had been when she'd appeared and fallen into Jules' arms. Somehow, her clothing hadn't made it to the seventeenth century — if that was where she was — but the scroll had.

And where's Bree?

Jules didn't remember anything after stepping through the portal. Except her kidnapper shoving her into his shirt and kissing her.

She scanned the beach, but they were moving fast now that he had her again.

Like he doesn't want to chance a round two.

Jules couldn't see anything but the rolling waves of the ocean to their right and rocky sandy terrain that bled into grassy hills up ahead.

If she really had traveled through time, the Isle of Skye didn't look much different.

"Weeeel?" he prompted. "Dinnae be able ta speak now?"

She didn't let his thick brogue roll over her body. Totally ignored its appeal, too. He was a barbarian who'd grabbed her, smacked her ass, and hauled her around like a rag doll. Not to mention, kissed her.

The bastard.

Breath exited her mouth on a whoosh. "I—"

The big horse slowed, and the man nudged her shoulder. "Ye, wha', lass?"

More '*lass*,' just like in modern-day Scotland.

Jules *hated* that she preferred when this guy said it. She shook her head. "You wouldn't believe me if I told you."

I traveled back in time. Actually did it. Magic is real.

She trembled.

"Cold?"

"No." His body heat at her back was keeping Jules warm, staving off the goose bumps on her legs from rising higher. She'd cooled off from her run, but her heart still pounded. As much as she hated to admit it, she was cozy in the barbarian's unyielding embrace. She wouldn't tell him that, though. "What year is it?" Jules blurted.

"The year of our Lord, sixteen hundred and seventy-five."

Three years off…

"Claire came to 1672." She spoke more to herself than him, but her captor cocked his head to one side—she felt more than saw it.

"So, yer parchment said."

"Magic," she whispered.

He didn't comment.

Jules wanted to ask him a hundred things, or demand to know where they were going. She needed to make a plan to find her sister. Then get them home, damn the nonsense about love and marriage. Claire—and Jules—belonged in the twenty-first century.

She'd have to work on getting away from the barbarian first. Then find Bree. Jules was going to need the Irish chick to get home.

They rode for a long time, neither of them talking. Which was fine with Jules, because she was busy formulating a plan.

"We're almost there." He broke the silence sometime later.

"Where's *there?*"

"Armadale."

She'd heard that name before. The bartender, Rob MacDonald had told her his clan's stronghold was in ruins—at least in the twenty-first century. "MacDonald."

The man stilled. "Aye. Ye know a' me?"

Jules glanced over her shoulder and shook her head. "I know Armadale is the stronghold of Clan MacDonald."

"Aye. My clan." His tone bled pride.

Her heart skipped. Her mind ran in circles. Websites, books, magazine articles flashed before her eyes, and Jules didn't like the math her head was doing. Clans MacDonald and MacLeod were rivals—enemies.

They'd been at war—*real war*—not even a century before the seventeenth.

How did we end up three years off target?

Never mind that…

If Claire's letter was at all true, Jules had fallen into the hands of her sister's husband's enemy.

She swallowed a gulp. Fear skittered up her belly, sliding down her arms and legs. Her pulse thundered in her temples.

What's he going to do to me?

Police training fled as the reality of what she'd done—*where she was*—settled over her. Jules was almost naked, without a weapon, and in the arms of a man who'd already proven he had a savage streak.

He'd chased her down after she'd punched him in the nuts.

What kind of revenge will he seek?

"Please don't hurt me." The words tumbled from her mouth, and she shook in his grip. She twisted around to look at him.

"Who said anythin' abou' hurtin' ye?" The man reared back. Looked insulted.

"My sister married a MacLeod."

He chuckled. "Poor lass."

When their eyes met, the satisfaction she read there pushed away her fear, reigniting her anger.

This guy's a pompous ass.

Jules frowned. She should probably rejoice he didn't seem angry anymore—about the punch or the chasing.

However, he was ticking *her* off.

"Ah, there's tha' fire I like. Glare a' me, lass. Ye dinnae be weak."

She narrowed her eyes. "If you're not going to hurt me, what *do* you plan to do to me?"

Those dark eyes flashed, and Jules' stomach fluttered.

When his lips parted, her heart kicked up another notch.

She remembered his mouth moving over hers against her will. His hands at her waist—then on her bare thighs.

If Jules hadn't been so out of it, she wouldn't have

kissed him back.

Stranger or not, the guy could kiss.

I've lost it.

Maybe time travel-induced insanity.

Since when am I attracted to pushy bastards?

No. Way.

Not even if the circumstances were different. This guy's nowhere near my type.

He said nothing, but she couldn't stop staring at him.

The barbarian stared right back.

The horse kept walking, paying neither of them any attention.

Her kidnapper's five o'clock shadow begged for her touch. Her fingers twitched in his grip.

Okay.

Seriously?

Knock it off, Juliette McGowan.

"I'll tell the MacLeods I hold ye captive."

She jumped when he finally spoke. "C-c-captive?"

"Aye. Yer fer ransom."

chapter six

"Ransom?"

"I know ye dinnae be daft, lass, so why're ye repeatin' everythin' I say?" Hugh bit back a chuckle when she glared harder, and those green eyes flashed.

This lass was a fascinating contradiction of strength and weakness, and he wanted her.

Burned for her.

You've gone mad, Hugh MacDonald.

Chasing her had fired his blood, despite the pain that'd rocked his tender parts when she'd hit him. His cock had twitched when he'd swept her up into his arms, so at least it still worked—praise Jesus.

He'd almost put her on Dubh's back facing him so he could kiss her again. Holding her against his chest wasn't a chore, even though he was restraining her.

"Screw you," she bit out, breaking their eye-contact.

The phrase was odd, but he got the gist of her meaning. "Ye offerin'?" He *should* tell her how badly he wanted her. Then she wouldn't speak to him as such. *No one* showed him the disrespect this lass was.

What would she say if I told her?

By way of answer, she pounded his thigh with a tight fist and Hugh laughed.

"I'm glad you think this shit is funny. Just let me go. I want to go to the MacLeods anyway. I'll find my way to Dunvegan. You won't even miss me. Let me do what I came here to do."

He didn't blink an eye at her vulgarity; he admired her ability to speak her mind. His fascination with her shot up a notch. "And just wha' is *tha'*, exactly?"

She froze, as if she realized she'd said more than she'd wanted to. "None of your business," his foundling bit out finally.

Her neck and cheeks were stained pink, and Hugh couldn't stop staring.

"It's not like you're gonna help me," she mumbled, tugging against his hold.

"What're ye called?" Words fell out of his dry mouth. He cleared his throat.

"Why?"

"I've ta put a name to my demands, dinnae?"

The lass leaned away from him as much as she could, a scowl marring her pretty face.

It just made him want to kiss her even more.

"Demands?" she barked.

"Shall I go first?"

"What if I don't care what your name is?" she snapped.

Hugh threw his head back and laughed. "I like ye, lass."

"Well, I don't like you." She harrumphed and it took all he was made of not to grab her face and suck on that plump bottom lip.

"I'm The MacDonald."

She scoffed. "Like the only one?"

"Nay. Laird of my clan. My given name is Hugh."

"Great. I'm stuck with the Chief of the Barbarians." Her voice was low, more to herself than to him.

Hugh couldn't stop grinning. "Aye."

"Perfect."

"Aye, 'tis quite."

"Obviously sarcasm is lost on you, *Hugh*."

He should've chide her for being so casual with his name, but Hugh liked the sound of it on her lips. Hell, he liked her lips….and tasting them. His cock stirred and he shifted on Dubh's back.

If she realized what she was doing to him, his little lass would be even angrier. He wanted to keep her calm. He was enjoying their conversation.

So, he banished his desire — for now — and met her gaze when she looked his way again.

"And ye are…?"

"Pissed off."

"Odd name."

His foundling sighed. She cast her eyes skyward. "Jules."

"Jewels?"

"It's short for Juliette. Juliette McGowan. My name."

"Juliette." Her name rolled off his tongue smoothly, so he said it again. He liked it. A name as beautiful as she was.

She shivered in his grip.

Awareness shot down his spine and he couldn't muster a comment about her surname.

Juliette might be angry, but the lass was affected by him. It fired his blood—and his cock—in a way he didn't need right now.

"Don't say my name like you know me," she growled.

Hugh swallowed a groan. That tone, and the look on her face made heat shoot right to his crotch. He glanced down, catching sight of her bare upper thigh.

Seeing the expanse of creamy pale skin didn't cool his ardor, either. He didn't need a reminder that she was clad in *only* his tunic. Or remember what she looked like beneath it.

Juliette squirmed and he held her tighter, nestled against his chest. Hugh needed her to sit still. She was too close to his bollocks to not notice his interest. Friction was a bad thing.

"Dinnae matter if I ken ye, as ye say."

I still want you.

He cleared his throat again as his stomach flipped.

"How do you know the MacLeods will care enough to pay a ransom for me anyway?"

"As ye said, yer sister married a MacLeod."

"So? They don't know *me*."

"They'll pay ta have ye safely returned, dinnae fash."

Juliette stilled, that green gaze sought his over her shoulder. "I thought you said you weren't going to hurt me."

"I dinnae."

She frowned.

Hugh grinned. "They dinnae ken that."

His foundling narrowed her eyes but said nothing.

She muttered something under her breath he didn't catch.

He didn't goad her into talking to him. Hugh could feel her ire, but also her uncertainty, and a part of him didn't want to scare her. He was pleased she was strong and not afraid of him.

Armadale came into view and caught her attention. Juliette stared at his vast, glorious home up ahead, as if fascinated. Her eyes trailed the wall, the battlements, the gates, everything.

Hugh wanted to puff his chest out with pride and tell her everything about Clan MacDonald at the same time.

The longer she stared in silence, the more he realized she wasn't admiring his home. Her gaze was calculating, as if she was planning an escape route.

He was torn between laughter and admiration. "The Highlands are full of brigands and thieves. Lasses dinnae do well on their own."

Juliette harrumphed. "I was doing just fine on my

own."

"Aye. Naked an' confused on the beach. I thought ye were in yer cups."

She harrumphed again. "I would've figured something out."

"In tha' case, I should leave ye ta go abou' yer way."

They approached the gates, and Hugh nodded to his guards. They were blood-kin, and both clad in MacDonald plaids.

Juliette's gaze was shrewd as they rode into the bailey. "I don't believe that for a second. Not after all the trouble you went to, catching me and all."

Hugh threw his head back and laughed.

His cousin Colin looked at him as if he'd grown a third eye.

He ignored the man three years his junior and slid from Dubh's back. Hugh reached for his feisty foundling.

"Don't touch me," Juliette barked as his hands enclosed her waist.

All the MacDonalds about the courtyard stopped their tasks, suddenly interested in their laird's activities.

For some reason he wanted to snarl at all his kinsmen for looking at Juliette's nearly bare form.

"My laird?" Colin asked.

"Mind yer duties," he barked.

His cousin inclined his head and returned to the

gate as Hugh pinned a protesting Juliette to his chest.

"Let me go, or I'll scream."

"Scream away, lass. We're surrounded by my kinsmen. I'm laird. No one will pay ye notice."

However, they *were*.

All his clansmen—and women—were staring.

"Great, you're *all* barbarians?" Her question was part demand, part plea.

Hugh strode forward, giving her the choice to walk with him or get dragged.

Her struggles echoed in the great hall, but he didn't bother hushing her. Soon they'd be in his quarters, and then Hugh could—

"Hugh? Who've ye go' there?"

He froze, one foot on the wide staircase.

"Help!" Juliette hollered, renewing her efforts to jerk against his hold.

His aunt shuffled over, her cane making a *tap-tap* on the stone as she hurried faster than her uneven legs should be able to carry her.

Any concern for her health dissolved when he met her dark eyes—and her scowl.

A look that would have made him tremble if he was still a lad.

"Hugh MacDonald, who is tha' lass?"

"No one of yer concern, Auntie."

"Help, he's kidnapped me!" Juliette yelled. Her nails bit into his wrists.

Hugh growled and swung her up over his

shoulder, giving her delectable bare bottom a slap in the hopes the shock would silence her.

Juliette yelped and pounded his back with both fists.

Aunt Mab gasped. "Upstairs, lad. Now. Explain yerself!"

He groaned.

"Yer goin' ta *wha'*?"

Jules wanted to peek around the corner and see whoever was yelling at Hugh, despite the fact he'd barked at her to stay put. Delight bubbled up from her stomach. "Looks like someone's bigger and badder than you, Hugh MacDonald."

The *someone* was female.

She sucked back a giggle.

Wait…female?

What if he was married?

"He…kissed me." Elation dissipated and Jules screamed at herself. "I wouldn't care if he was married." Besides, no seventeenth century woman would talk to her husband like that. Definitely not a husband like Hugh.

His mom?

No.

He'd called her *Auntie* before they'd come upstairs. Jules hadn't gotten a good look at her though, not with all the shifting against Hugh's chest and her hair in her face when she'd been upside down over his shoulder.

She ignored the memories of his big hands on her ass and thighs. His touch was hot, burning her though he still hadn't hurt her.

Jules shivered and chided herself. She planted her hands on her thighs and leaned forward, trying to make out the screaming conversation in the corridor. Listening to the big strong barbarian backpedalling was kinda funny.

Conversation was no longer the right term.

Hugh raised his voice when his aunt did.

"Shouting match." Jules grinned and shook her head.

Both had thick brogues, so she couldn't make out every word, anyway.

She looked around the room as their voices faded in and out. Hugh had planted her on the bed. He'd barked, "Dinnae move," as he'd gone, rushing back out of the room, and slamming the thick door.

Two windows were open, heavy drapes tacked back. Light streamed into the sizable room, and the fire was lit in the big hearth, warm and inviting. Peat moss tickled her nose, but the scent was earthy and inviting as it wafted through the air.

There wasn't much inside; the stone walls were empty, save for a painting on the far wall she was too far from to inspect. It was a fair-haired woman, but that was all Jules could make out.

The whole place had Hugh written all over it—sparsely decorated. Masculine. What little furniture was oversized dark wood, including the huge bed she was seated on.

I'm in his bed.

Jules looked at the four carved posters and large headboard. It was made for a king, complete with fluffy-looking pillows and plaid blanket under her ass.

She pictured Hugh, naked and spread out all over this bed, sheets mussed. If his bare chest was any indication, the rest of him would look fantastic, too.

Gawd, knock it off.

Why are you playing Stockholm-Syndrome-Girl?

Jules rubbed her arms when tremors chased each other down her spine. Just because he looked good, didn't mean he was. So far, her acquaintance with him proved that, if nothing else.

Hugh MacDonald was *all* barbarian, no matter what the packaging looked like.

The door swung open, hitting the stone wall hard.

She winced and jumped.

"Lass, are ye hurt?" A little old lady shuffled forward, leaning heavily on a wood cane and walking fast enough to make her pant. Her awkward gait didn't seem to impede her step as she closed the distance to the bed.

Jules shot to her feet, worried the elderly lady would trip and fall. She tugged Hugh's shirt down as far as she could but didn't take her eyes off his aunt.

"Ye can wipe tha' look off yer face." The woman straightened and drummed her fingers on the top of the cane. "I am well. 'Tis ye I'm concerned wit'."

"I'm okay." She stumbled over the words, feeling heat scorch the back of her neck as the woman's eyes trailed her frame.

"Talk oddly, ye do."

Hugh came into the room, his arms crossed over that broad — and still bare — chest. The look on his face was as dark as his eyes. "Auntie —"

"Ye an' I are finished speakin', Hugh MacDonald."

Jules arched an eyebrow.

The older woman's tone was hard as nails, to match the glare she threw at him. However, her expression softened when she looked back at Jules.

Hugh hovered like a socially inept teenager. Practically in the corner.

Jules was torn between looking at her suddenly humbled barbarian and the woman who was appraising her.

"Pay no heed ta the lad. I'll call fer Rhona and get ye some clothin'."

The lad?

Hugh had to be at least thirty.

Jules tried not to snort when he shifted from one boot to the other at the end of his bed.

He said nothing, but he wore his brooding like a shroud.

"Lass, are ye hungry? I'll have a bath drawn as

well."

"No. I'm fine. Don't go to trouble over me, please. I'll take the clothing, though."

The woman smiled, taking years from her wrinkled face. "Ye dinnae be trouble." She pointed to Hugh with her cane. "This one, on t'other hand, is nothin' but."

"Amen, sister," Jules muttered.

Hugh threw her a black look, although there was no way he'd know what her phrase meant.

"I'm Mab, this one's aunt. I raised 'im up, I did."

"I'm Jules." She didn't mind giving her name to the woman who could put her barbarian in check.

Mab paused, cocking her head to one side.

"It's short for Juliette." She smiled at Hugh's aunt.

"Bonnie name, bonnie lass." Mab circled her body, looking her up and down.

Jules squirmed, chiding herself to stand still. "Thank you," she managed.

"No' from 'round here, are ye?"

"No." Jules sought Hugh's gaze for some reason.

Her barbarian gave a slight nod.

"I'm from the future."

He straightened those broad shoulders and dropped his arms as Jules voiced what she hadn't said aloud even during their *civil* conversation on his horse's back.

"The future?" Mab asked.

chapter seven

both MacDonalds listened intently as she explained meeting Bree and coming back in time. They didn't even look at her like she was crazy when she told them Claire had come back before her.

Jules didn't admit she'd come to grab her sister and get home, but she'd already confirmed to Hugh Claire had married Duncan MacLeod.

He wasn't stupid. Could probably put two and two together. His shrewd gaze watched her as she spoke.

Mab kept nodding and cocked her head to one side as she listened. Her long salt and pepper hair fell over one shoulder. It was bound but coming loose. "The Fae are nothin' but trouble," she declared finally.

"But you believe me?" Jules asked.

"Aye."

Hugh was quiet as he regarded her.

No matter how Jules tried to avoid his dark eyes, she couldn't.

Their gazes collided over and over.

Mab looked at her nephew. "On the morrow, ye'll take the lass ta Dunvegan."

"Nay. Juliette is my prisoner," Hugh growled.

The older woman glared and struggled to her feet. Mab faced her nephew, cane poised like a weapon. "Nay. Dinnae be daft, lad. I will no' let ye start another war wit' Clan MacLeod. We've peace. We're goin' ta keep it tha' way."

He glowered from his seat next to the fireplace. "There's nay harm in a little ransom. I dinnae defile or wed Juliette, as was done in years past."

Jules snorted. "Damn straight you won't." However, she had to swallow a gulp.

He'd been completely serious.

She'd read that rape and forced marriages were common—and accepted by society when a woman was stolen for ransom. Clan law was paramount. Consequences for non-payment were high—and final. Not even the kings had really bossed Highlanders around. Each clan was pretty much like its own little kingdom.

Neither MacDonald even spared her a glance. Their eyes—and glares—were deadlocked on each other.

"I am yer laird."

"And I wiped yer arse."

Jules laughed; she couldn't help it. "Sorry," she muttered when Hugh turned his scowl in her direction. However, she'd inadvertently broken the tension.

Mab waved the cane in her direction and smiled. "I like this lass." She patted her shoulder.

Jules flashed a smile for the old lady. "Thanks,

you're not so bad yourself."

Hugh's aunt's face crinkled as she returned a grin.

He harrumphed and leaned back in his chair; arms crossed over his broad chest.

Shame he'd found a new shirt. Barbarian or not, he was nice to look at.

"Did ye think ta ask tha lass wha' she wants?" Mab asked.

"Dinnae be my concern. She's a captive."

Jules rolled her eyes. "What if I run away?"

"Ye'll nay last a day out there on yer own, let alone find yer way ta the MacLeods." He pitched his big body forward, dark eyes daring her.

"Try me." Jules glared.

Hugh chuckled and shook his head. "I'm keepin' her."

"Ye. Are. No'." Mab punctuated each word of her shout by ramming her cane to the stone floor with a *thud*.

"Dinnae try me, old woman. I am yer laird." His tone was hard, and Hugh narrowed his eyes at his aunt.

Jules fidgeted and sat straighter on the huge bed.

Mab had wrapped her in a MacDonald tartan with the promise of clothing when they were done speaking.

Her heart skipped and she sucked in a breath. For some reason, she was nervous, but not really afraid.

"Dinnae be daft. Think on it, Hugh. Peace wit' the MacLeods has been long awaited. Yer da did tha' right if nothin' else. Dinnae risk yer clan. Yer life. Fer one lass."

Should I be insulted?

Mab shot her a glance, as if she'd read her mind. "I mean nay insult, lass. My nephew's stubborn, but he's a good laird. He'll do the righ' thing. Ye dinnae be a captive. Dinnae fash."

"She *is* a captive." Despite his words, Hugh's voice lost some steam and his big shoulders loosened.

Jules could see he realized his aunt was right, even if he wouldn't say it out loud. She was torn between chiding him and admiring his resolve. He certainly hadn't let go of the tough guy routine.

Mab scoffed and shook her head. She met Jules' eyes. "Come, lass, we'll get ye somethin' ta wear and food in yer belly."

"She stays here wit' me," Hugh barked.

Jules rolled her eyes.

He's totally pouting now.

His aunt opened her mouth to speak, but Jules beat the old lady to it.

"Fine, my laird. As long as you promise to take me to Claire in the morning. I'll even promise not to run away." Maybe if she threw in his title and made him think she respected him, he'd agree.

"Ye dinnae get far." That dark gaze raked her face and Jules' stomach flipped.

She chided herself not to wiggle on the bed or squeeze her thighs tight as she was inclined. There wasn't anything remotely sexual about the way he was looking at her, yet her body tingled.

All over.

Jules wanted to roll her eyes at herself.

Knock it off. He's still your kidnapper.

Hugh relaxed in the chair and grunted.

Mab clapped her gnarled hands. "'Tis settled then. Juliette is our guest."

He said nothing, but his eyes spoke volumes. Hugh disagreed with his aunt's take on things.

Jules fought the urge to gulp.

What does that *mean for me?*

The door was thrown open, and Hugh didn't pause to catch it before it slammed into the wall. He said nothing as he shoved it shut moments later.

The *thud* made Jules jump.

He prowled toward her, those big shoulders swaying as he went. He moved with grace for a guy his size, and his appeal was undeniable.

She had to swallow, then screamed at herself for it. Jules shifted her weight from foot to foot, unable to dart away as she should.

Her barbarian stopped a few feet from her, still silent as he appraised her. His long dark locks were wet and his clothing fresh. No sword was belted to his waist, either.

Sandalwood and peat tickled her nose.

Hugh must have bathed.

Awareness crackled in the air between them, and Jules felt naked, despite the yards of fabric that made up the chemise Mab had given her. It was thick and off-white, with a high neckline and long puffy sleeves all the way to her wrists. It fell to her feet, too, so there was no way he could see any of her body. She had nothing beneath it since underwear was pretty scarce in the seventeenth century.

Hugh would know that.

The gown was heavy and hot; she was already starting to sweat; despite the bath she'd had.

He closed the distance between them, still saying nothing. He snaked an arm around her waist and pulled Jules close.

"What are you doing?" The words were supposed to be a demand but left her lips as a breathless whisper that made her curse herself to hell and back.

Those dark eyes bored into hers, and her mouth went dry.

She couldn't tug out of his arms. Could feel his heart beating steadily against hers.

His mouth crashed down on hers, and Jules moved into him instead of away.

When Hugh slanted for a deeper kiss, she met his tongue with hers. Warmth spread across her chest, slid down her belly and settled between her legs. Her sex bloomed, yet he hadn't touched her anywhere near there.

Big hands slipped down her back, cupping her bottom. Hugh pinned her to his chest when her thighs quivered, and it was a damn good thing, because Jules was melting. She'd be a puddle at his feet in moments.

All she could do was cling to him and kiss him back. He plundered her mouth, his tongue shoving against hers, pushing, and rubbing. Battling as if they were dueling.

Hugh kissed her until tingles darted all over her body, and Jules was a shivering mess of desire.

Every place with a nerve ending throbbed for more.

He was on the same page, if the hardness pressing into her stomach, was any indication.

She rested her palms against his hard pecs, her head spinning as their mouths moved together. Since when was she turned on by *a* kiss?

Was this a dream?

Wait.

This is no dream.

Sense started to descend, pushing the foolishness out of her brain. Hazy passion faded as she fought for coherent thought.

Hugh MacDonald is kissing me.

Jules gasped and yanked away from him.

Barbarian.

Kidnapper.

She panted, bending at the waist, and grabbing her knees so she wouldn't tumble to her ass. "Don't—" she had to clear her throat, "do that again."

His smile was slow and sexy — *damn* him.

"Ye dinnae be complainin' a few minutes ago." His lips were swollen and flushed red from hers and she couldn't look away.

Jules straightened and growled. "Don't touch me again. You won't like what happens."

"Oh aye? On tha contrary, I'd verra much like ta ken." Hugh took a step forward and reached for her, but she slid back, extending her arm.

"I'll kick you in the balls, for starters."

Hugh threw his head back and laughed. "Nay, lass. Ye dinnae."

She narrowed her eyes. "Try me."

"I plan ta *try* ye, as ye say."

"The hell you will. You won't get very far, except for a sore dick. Just leave me alone."

He shook his head, amusement darting all over his expression. He was genuinely delighted with her threats. Hugh looked carefree and hot as hell.

Jules pinned her fists to her sides so she wouldn't punch the look off his face.

He chuckled and grabbed her wrist. "The things ye say, lass."

She glared at the twinkle in his eyes.

He'd shaved — there was no stubble on his cheeks, and she wanted to drag her fingers against his skin.

Dammit.

Just stop it.

"Let me go," Jules ordered.

"I'll have ye in my bed."

She shook her head, but Hugh wrapped his arms around her and picked her up. Instead of tossing her over his shoulder, he held her like a baby against his hard chest and carried her to that oversized bed. His eyes bored into hers.

Fear chased away her ire. "Hugh." She wanted to demand he release her, but the words wouldn't form. He was bigger and stronger, as he'd proven all day long.

What if he wants to rape me?

"Juliette." His voice was a whisper and he set her down with surprising gentleness.

Jules scrambled to the headboard and hugged her knees to her chest.

Hugh paused, arching an eyebrow. "I dinnae hurt ye."

"I don't want to have sex with you," she blurted.

He cocked his head to one side. "Ye want me, lass."

"No." Jules' denial was too quick—and they both knew it.

His shoulders loosened and he joined her on the bed. Hugh moved toward her, and Jules' pulse thundered in her ears.

She didn't look away from his eyes. She couldn't.

Hugh cupped her cheeks. "I dinnae intend ta force ye, Juliette. Ne'er that."

"Thank you," Jules whispered. Her heart pounded

as his hands fell away from her face. She slowly unfolded her body and lay down, but she couldn't relax.

Waited for Hugh to do or say something.

Anything.

Her barbarian extended his big body in the bed, pulling the blankets higher, covering them both. One corner of his mouth shot up. "Ye want me, lass. Dinnae matter what yer sayin' now."

Jules' stomach fluttered but she didn't dare answer. She might agree. "I'm leaving tomorrow. Like you promised."

Hugh grinned and dragged his hand down her arm.

She trembled, even though he hadn't touched bare skin. "I *am* going, Hugh."

"I'm a man a' my word, lass. I'll see ye ta Dunvegan. But, when tha time is righ', ye'll return ta me. And there dinnae be a need ta force ye. Ye'll come ta my bed willin'. I'll have ye, Juliette."

Jules gulped at the promise in his eyes, in his voice. She stared as he turned over, settling his head deep into a thick pillow, his dark hair fanned out.

She didn't move as she watched him.

Soon, Hugh's breathing became deep and even, but Jules couldn't loosen her body or concentrate on much-needed sleep. She was tense, gripping the MacDonald plaid with both hands as she tugged it to her chin.

Crushing her eyes shut, all she could see, remember...*feel* was his mouth moving over hers.

Jules cursed and sucked in a breath.

It's gonna be a long night.

chapter eight

When he rolled over, he remembered he wasn't in bed alone. Hugh swallowed a yawn as he came around and blinked to clear his vision. The room was dim, but not wholly dark and he could see a sea of honey waves spread on his pillow.

Her face was turned toward his as she slept, and he restrained himself from touching her.

Hugh didn't want to let her go.

He'd promised his aunt he wouldn't ransom her, but could he keep Juliette some other way?

She'd kissed him back when he'd stormed into his rooms after his bath in the stables.

The fear in her eyes had given him pause. She'd actually thought he'd rape her.

Hugh growled.

He'd never forced himself on a lass, no matter how many lovers he'd taken since —

Still couldn't say her name.

His eyes instinctively avoided the blasted painting that hung in the corner by the fireplace. Every time he'd taken it down, someone — probably his Aunt Mab — had returned it to the spot it'd been in since he'd gotten married eleven years before.

As if he needed assistance with his guilt.

Juliette stirring washed the dismal memories from his head—thank Jesus.

She moaned as she stretched, arching her back, and Hugh stilled, unable to rip his gaze away. She was temptation alive, and he fought a shudder and the heat that settled in his groin.

"Lass, ye—"

Her beautiful green eyes flew open, and she froze. "Oh my God."

Hugh quirked an eyebrow.

She shook her head. "Dammit."

"Somethin' wrong?" He propped himself on one elbow, looked down at her and restrained himself from doing more than *looking*.

Juliette's cheeks were flushed pink, and her body was sleep-warmed. Hugh wanted to reach for her. Touch her.

Then take her.

"Everything is wrong. I *am* here. It wasn't some horrible nightmare." She snorted and sat up, scooting away from him. "Odd, that I'd wish for a nightmare, but I'd rather have night terrors than be here."

Hugh frowned and stroked her cheek; he couldn't help it. "Am I so bad?"

She leaned away, her familiar glare back in place. "Yes."

He didn't know whether to admire her resolve or

let the insult inching up from his gut take over. "Weeeel, I am glad ta wake an' find ye in my bed."

Juliette narrowed her eyes. "I told you I wouldn't run away. You just have to come through with your end of the bargain."

"I'm a man a' my word."

She studied him, saying nothing. The golden waves of her hair kissed her shoulders, disheveled from sleep.

His fingers itched to smooth them and taste her lush lips again. Perhaps she'd even kiss him back like last night.

"Don't look at me like that," Juliette snapped.

Hugh startled, forcing a breath, and reclining into his carved headboard. The bite of wood at his shoulders was refreshing. His cock twitched and he was glad for the blankets still covering him.

Aye, I am insulted.

No lass he'd ever pursued had refused his advances.

Was that why he was so intrigued with this one?

He pushed off the wood behind him and shot to his knees, leaning toward Juliette. Intentionally towering over her. Hugh blocked her in, resting his palms against the headboard.

Instead of the fear he'd seen in that emerald gaze the night before, anger darted across her countenance. "Get away from me."

"Nay." Hugh grinned. "Before I take ye ta yer

sister, ye will admit ye want me."

"No, I won't."

"Ye dinnae want me, or ye dinnae admit it?"

"I hate to break it to ya, dude. You're far from God's gift to women."

Her phrasing was odd, and he had no idea what *dude* meant, but the rest of her statement was clear. Hugh threw his head back and laughed. He'd assure her he'd never had complaints, but it would only rouse more ire. He liked her feisty, but he enjoyed her company. Wanted to talk to her more.

Juliette shoved him backwards, both palms to his chest. She scooted from his bed before he could react, but Hugh threw his palms flat behind him and avoided falling on his arse — barely.

"Get out of here so I can get dressed." His foundling perched both hands on her shapely hips, but the sleeping gown still hid too much of her form.

Not that Hugh had any trouble remembering her naked on the beach. More heat shot to his groin, and he swallowed. He slid his legs over the side of his bed and stood, then stalked to her. "Nay. *I* am the laird, an' these are *my* rooms. Ye dinnae put me ou'."

She frowned. "Fine. At least turn around."

"Why?" Hugh smiled.

Juliette huffed and whirled away, grabbing a tunic — not a more feminine leine — Mab must've left for her. Instead of skirts, there was a pair of folded trews beneath them.

Why would his aunt get her lad's clothing?

There were skirts and gowns in the stores, surely.

He stayed close, restraining himself from wrapping his arms around her; Hugh contented himself by brushing her hair from her shoulder. He leaned down, kissing the skin below her ear he'd exposed, and cursing the high neckline of the chemise she wore.

She shivered. He saw it. Juliette couldn't hide it from him. She didn't move away, either.

"I'm waitin', lass."

Juliette whirled on him. He didn't miss her white knuckled grip on the saffron tunic. "You're gonna be *waitin'* a long time. I. Don't. Want. *You.*"

Undeterred, Hugh stepped forward and dragged two fingers down her cheek. "Ye dinnae be honest, Juliette."

She swallowed and he wanted to kiss her throat. "I am." However, her words shook. "Just let me get dressed and I'll leave. Be out of your hair. You won't have to worry about me anymore."

"I'm thinkin' I'll keep ye." Hugh reached for her chemise, undoing the top two buttons on the neck.

"No." Juliette flashed him a black look and batted his hands away. "You promised."

"Ye dinnae let me finish." He let her shove him away and straightened, swallowing a smile because it would make her even angrier.

"What?" She arched a fair eyebrow, her expression

shouting distrust.

"Stay wit' me one more day."

"Why?" Juliette cocked her head to one side.

"I want ye, lass."

"One day isn't going to make me fall into your bed with my legs open."

Hugh chuckled and reached for her.

She wasn't quick enough to evade him, and he plastered her to his chest.

He inhaled her sweetness instead of kissing her like he wanted to. Juliette smelled like the floral soap women of his clan always bathed with. Making it was his aunt's specialty.

"Let me go, Hugh." Her voice was whisper, not demand. She trembled against him, the saffron tunic an unfortunate obstacle to feeling her breasts against his chest. The thick fabric, along with Juliette's hands, were pinned against him.

"Nay."

They stared at each other, and silence fell.

"I dinnae hurt ye," he said finally.

"I know." Juliette swallowed again, but her voice was steady.

She believes me.

Hugh ignored how his stomach flipped. "Stay another day."

"Is that an order?"

"Aye."

Juliette frowned. "For the record, I won't sleep

with you."

"Ye did sleep wit' me." Hugh smiled.

She pursed her lips. "You know what I mean. I won't have sex with you, Hugh MacDonald. I mean it. We just met, and I don't do that sorta thing."

"Are ye innocent then?"

"You mean, am I a virgin?"

Hugh nodded.

"No, not for a long time."

"Are ye wed?" His gut clenched as he awaited her answer, but he banished that foolishness.

"I was once." Juliette gazed up at him. He couldn't read her expression, or the emotions that darted across those eyes.

"I am sorry fer yer loss, then."

She shook her head, her golden locks shifting with the movement. "He didn't die. He cheated. I caught him in bed with another woman, so I left. We divorced. You know that term?"

Hugh nodded. "Aye. 'Tis no' somethin' oft done, but I ken of it."

"It doesn't matter. It was a long time ago. I moved on." Juliette averted her gaze.

Hugh wanted to tilt her chin up to force her to meet his eyes, but he didn't. If she was having a moment of pain, she needed to move past it on her own. Wasn't any of his concern, really. "I was wed once, as well." He cursed the dose of honesty that fell from his mouth.

Why did you say that?

Her eyes were wide when she looked back up at him. "What happened?" Her question was innocent and held no malice, but it was Hugh's turn to avert his gaze.

He released her so fast she stumbled, but he couldn't reach to steady her.

Juliette frowned—he could see it in his peripheral vision, but the painting in the corner was suddenly glaring.

It took all his attention, even though he didn't dare look at it.

"Hugh?"

"She died." He didn't mean to bark the words, but he did.

"I'm sorry." Juliette sounded genuinely bothered and concerned for him.

Hugh needed to go. Couldn't bear to see pity in her eyes.

He couldn't spare her a glance to look upon her sincerity. Anger roiled over him, and he made tight fists at his sides.

Hugh couldn't muster a response, nor did he give in to the urge to close his eyes. His chest was tight, breathing painful. He strode from the room and slammed the door as soon as both feet were in the corridor.

Jules blinked. She stared at the closed door and her head spun. "What the hell just happened?" She looked down at the yellow shirt in her hands and had to take one — then another — breath to clear her head.

Her barbarian had gone from fire to ice in about two seconds. He'd almost dropped her on her ass, too.

"Bipolar much?"

Not that she'd wanted him panting over her, anyway. Or trying to kiss her again. Which he hadn't — thank God.

Well except for the ones he'd planted on her neck that'd made her shiver.

Until he'd gone stiff as a board and cold. Harsh. Yanking away, as if she'd stung him.

What gives?

Hugh had been the one to start the twenty-question interrogation. She tried to shrug, but it bothered her more than she'd like to admit that he had feelings for another woman.

A dead woman.

I mean, he wouldn't have reacted that way if he didn't love her, right?

Jules sighed and slipped out of the chemise, shivering in the morning chill. There was no fire lit in the sizable hearth.

Whaddaya know, castles are drafty.

She tugged the shirt over her head, cursing at the lack of a bra. Her breasts were large; she needed support. They were going to ache by the end of the day.

The tunic fell mid-thigh, but *big* was okay with her. Hugh wouldn't be able to see her body so much. Maybe he'd stop touching her, too.

Jules ignored the little voice that protested the idea of her barbarian keeping his hands to himself.

His aunt had given in when she'd begged for pants instead of a skirt, but they were too big, too. Jules silently thanked her for the belt as she shoved it around her waist.

Finally dressed, she looked around the room. Morning light drifted in through the windows, and she went over, tugging the thick drapes open. The room brightened even more, looking less foreboding.

Hugh's stamp was all over the place. The room smelled like him, too, even though he was gone. Masculine spice that flipped her tummy and made her curse at herself.

Hmmm, that painting…

Jules had seen the picture the day before, but she hadn't taken time to study it. She crossed the room to check it out. Hugh had been so obviously ignoring it before he'd stomped away from her. As if he'd made *extra* efforts not to look in that corner.

A girl with long, pale blonde hair sat on a carved high-backed chair with her hands folded on her lap. Her gown was light green and elegant, with an embossed bodice, but it was modest. There was a plaid draped over her shoulder and wrapped around her waist, but it was a different pattern than the

MacDonald blanket on Hugh's bed.

She looked so damn young, and her brown eyes were solemn—too much so. Sad, maybe.

Brenna MacInnes was etched on a little plate on the bottom picture frame.

"That's Brenna. She was Hugh's lass." Mab's voice made Jules jump and curse. "Sorry, lass. Dinnae mean ta startle ye."

She hadn't heard Hugh's aunt enter the room. "It's okay." Jules forced a smile. "Good morning."

"'Mornin' ta ye, as well." Mab smiled and hobbled over with a heavy grip on her cane. It was worse than Jules had seen the night before. Maybe she was stiffer in the mornings. "Here ta check on ye. My lad came stormin' inta the hall. Are ye well?"

Jules smirked and nodded. "Yeah. He was…energetic this morning. Didn't much like that I wasn't."

Mab grinned, but then her wrinkled face sobered. "He dinnae hurt ye?"

"No, ma'am."

"Good. I'd have his hide."

Jules gave a small laugh. "Glad you have my back."

The old lady reached out and patted her hand. Silence fell as they both gazed up at the young girl in the painting.

A shiver shot down her spine.

Was Brenna's stare accusing?

As if she was demanding to know why Jules had spent the night in her husband's bed.

Jules straightened her shoulders and stood taller.

It's a painting. Stop being silly.

There was no change. Staring at Hugh's wife now was same as five minutes before. "She looks so sad." She managed a whisper, ignoring her paranoia.

"Aye, I expect she was upset when she sat for tha' painting. It proceeded her arrival ta Armadale. As a part of her dowry. Her father an' Hugh's were lads together. Clan MacInnes dinnae live too far off."

"Arranged marriage?"

Mab nodded. "As is tha way of most marriages 'round here."

"What happened?" Jules' stomach fluttered when she met the woman's dark eyes.

Her expression was saturated in sadness. "She died barin' his child. The Good Lord took the bairn, too." Mab made the sign of the cross and whispered something that wasn't English.

Jules frowned and swallowed against the emotion closing her throat.

Poor Hugh.

It explained a lot about who he was as a person.

Damaged. Just like me.

"'Twas a long time ago, lass. Dinnae look so sad." Mab grabbed her forearm and squeezed. "C'mon, let us go down ta the hall. Break yer fast, then I'll get one a' the lads ta take ye ta Dunvegan."

Jules' heart skipped a beat. "What? Hugh said he wanted me to stay another day."

Seriously?

Are you arguing?

Don't you want to go?

Mab cocked her head to one side. "My lad is gone on clan business. He asked me ta see ye safely ta yer sister."

Her stomach dropped. "He…left?"

If Hugh's aunt could sense her reaction, she hid it well, only offering a nod. "Aye, said he dinnae likely be back 'til tha morrow."

Jules nodded, but anger churned her gut.

Coward.

Her barbarian was a coward.

Something she'd never thought she'd be able to accuse him of.

Just wish I could say it to his face.

chapter nine

Jules couldn't help but look over her shoulder as she rode away from Armadale, Colin MacDonald's arms loosely around her.

So much for Hugh ordering me to stay another day.

Colin's hold was nothing like the laird's.

Was she crazy to miss Hugh's touch?

God. I've lost it for sure.

Hugh had run from her.

He hadn't even bothered to say goodbye. What a change from the guy who couldn't stop touching her. Kissing her.

Jules had grown used to him—well as much as a person could in so short a time—taking what he wanted no matter what she'd said.

She'd liked his kisses, as much as she *hated* that idea floating around in her head.

He must still love Brenna. So much he couldn't bear to look at me after talking about her.

Jules swallowed and tried not to fidget on the back of the big brown horse.

According to Mab, the girl had been dead almost eleven years.

He feels guilty for wanting me.

She harrumphed and squared her shoulders.

So what?

Jules didn't *want* him to want her. Certainly, didn't want *him*.

So why does it bother you now?

Because knowing he lost his wife and child made him just a little bit less of a bastard, a voice whispered.

Who could be normal *after that?*

"Never mind," Jules muttered.

It didn't matter. Not really.

Not being able to deal with loss didn't justify kidnapping. Or stolen kisses.

"My lady?" Colin's deep voice made her jump and her eyes darted to his. "Are ye well?" Blue eyes, so different from his cousin's, regarded her with concern.

Jules cleared her throat. "Yes. I'm okay. Thanks for asking."

He smiled and inclined his head. Colin was handsome, but the curve of his lips didn't make her stomach flutter or her heart patter like Hugh's.

She loved dark eyes. Always had.

Dammit.

Seriously. Stop. It.

She wasn't lusting after a barbarian, no matter how hot he *looked.*

Or how good his kisses were.

They rode in mostly silence for what felt like days but was probably just an hour or two.

Hugh's cousin didn't speak, which only resulted

in her obsessing. She couldn't get the laird out of her head. Or stop remembering how his kisses felt. Over and over.

Jules cringed. "H-h-how long until we get there?" *Stuttering? Really?*

If Colin noticed, his voice and expression didn't give it away. "Dinnae be much longer, my lady. Over tha' hill." He pointed up ahead.

She could already see the castle looming, so it was a wonder he didn't think her question was stupid, or snap at her for asking.

Hugh would've.

Jules rolled her eyes at herself for knowing her barbarian would've been a smartass about her nerves.

Knock it off, for reals, Juliette Ann McGowan.

Could one disown oneself?

She busied herself with memorizing the terrain, then screamed at herself for it. Like she needed to remember how to get back to Armadale.

She'd come for Claire.

Colin was taking her to Claire.

Then they could go home.

Again, they slipped back into silence, although it wasn't unpleasant. The closer they got to the MacLeod stronghold; the more Jules' nerves danced in her stomach.

Claire.

She was about to see her sister again.

"Halt!" The yell made Jules freeze in Colin's arms.

Shaking started when the guard jumped in front of the horse, a big sword drawn. He was blond and *huge*.

"MacDonald," he spat.

"Aye. Colin MacDonald. Cousin to the laird."

The big guy on the ground didn't look impressed.

Two more MacLeods—both wearing kilts and brandishing swords—flanked him.

"What do ye wan'?" The dark-haired one on the right hollered.

Jules straightened and met the brown eyes of the fair-haired guard. "Claire is my sister. I'm here…to see her."

Silence fell and the three guards stared.

The blond man slid forward; his face scrunched as he scrutinized. "Dismount," he barked.

She shot a look over her shoulder at Colin.

When Hugh's cousin nodded, Jules slid off the horse, accepting the helping hand of the blond guard to her biceps. He gripped but didn't hurt her.

"Ye've the look a' her."

Jules had been told that her whole life. "We're only a few years apart." Four to be exact, but he wouldn't care even if she'd explained. "Can I see her, please?"

The blond man looked at Colin without answering. "Get off MacLeod lands, MacDonald."

She shivered at his harsh voice.

"Dinnae harm the lass," Colin barked.

"*We* dinnae harm lasses." Another of the guards answered, eyes narrowed.

Colin snarled.

Harsh words were exchanged on both sides. As well as some posturing with swords and puffed chests.

Jesus. These guys are worse than a buncha cops.

It only took her a few moments to catch on to what the fuss was about. It was more than a dick-measuring contest. They were all referring to the debacle of Margaret MacLeod being sent home naked, in disgrace—as well as burned—after a botched marriage to the MacDonald laird.

God, it was almost a hundred years ago—this time, anyway. Mab wasn't kidding about anything *being a war threat.*

Jules shot forward when Colin drew his sword.

She waved her arms. "Boys! I just wanna see my sister. Colin, I'm fine with these guys. Go back to Armadale. Tell Hugh..." she cleared her throat. "Tell Hugh thank you and that I'm okay here. Thank *you* for bringing me."

Silence fell and all four men outside the gates stared at her.

Finally—*finally*—Colin sheathed his sword and nodded. "I'll tell the laird yer in safe hands."

"Thank you," Jules whispered.

The three MacLeod guards didn't relax, nor did they open the gates, until after Colin was a speck on the horizon.

When Jules met the big blond guy's eyes, he laughed.

She arched a brow. "What's funny?"

"Yer strong, like yer sister. Like a MacLeod lass. Ye'll fit 'round here just fine."

Jules smirked. "Good."

Won't be here long enough to matter.

"I'm Cormac, head of tha guards, and cousin ta the laird. These two are Braedon and Jamie, my brothers."

She nodded, muttered polite greetings, and met the dark-haired guards, even though she was antsy. Jules shifted from foot to foot in the boots Mab had gotten her. The only part of her wardrobe that fit.

I want to see Claire. Now.

"Come, lass, I'll take ye ta yer sister," Cormac said, gesturing as the other two started to open the wide gates.

"You read my mind, dude."

Keeping up with his long legs was a chore that kept Jules at a jog, but soon she was walking into a great hall bigger than the one at Armadale.

A familiar blonde was near the largest hearth — one of three — with her back to them, rocking something in her arms.

Even with her back facing Jules, she *knew* her sister.

Claire was before her.

"My lady." Cormac's deep voice echoed.

Slowly Claire turned, a smile in place that faded when her eyes rested on Jules. "Jules?"

The incredulity in her sister's tone made Jules'

heart skip.

"Claire-bear," she breathed. The childhood nickname slipped out and Jules crossed the distance between them, running.

Cormac said something, but Jules tuned him out. Maybe Claire thanked him. Soon, the big guy bowed and was gone.

The dark-haired baby on Claire's hip took Jules' attention — the *something* — her sister was rocking by the warm fire.

He was adorable, with curls at the back of his little head. Big blue eyes dominated his chubby-cheeked face, but Jules saw Claire all over him. His little nose, the shape of those big eyes. Even his lips looked like her sister's.

Her heart plummeted to her stomach.

My baby sister has a kid.

"Jules. Jules. Jules." Her name was a chant. "What? How? Are you really here?" Claire's words fell out of her mouth on fast-forward.

Jules laughed; it was just like her sister.

And damn good to hear.

She threw her arms around her shorter sister but tried to be mindful of the baby.

"I can't believe you're really here," Claire whispered into Jules' shoulder.

Jules smiled as she got a whiff of clean baby. She reached out and stroked his downy hair.

Instead of being afraid of the stranger in his face,

the little guy flashed a smile that Claire echoed when their eyes met.

"This is Lachlan," her sister said, beaming now.

"He's beautiful, little sister." Jules stroked the baby's arm. "I have a nephew. How old is he?"

"Eighteen months. We're trying for number two." Her sister's cheeks were tinted pink, and she pressed a kiss to her son's forehead.

Jules' heart started to thunder in her ears. "Claire, I came for you."

Her sister frowned. "Came for me?"

"Yeah. To bring you home."

Claire stared, green eyes that matched Jules' own raking her face. "Didn't you read my letter?"

"I did, but—"

Her sister shook her head, making her blonde hair shift. Claire had always kept her locks on the long side, but her hair was longer than Jules had ever seen it. Down to her waist. She was dressed right out of a period movie—in a long olive skirt, ivory puffy-sleeved tunic with a lighter green corset over it. The colors brought out her eyes. She looked gorgeous.

"There's no buts, Jules."

"Claire—"

"Claire!" A deep booming voice took their collective attention. A huge guy with long dark hair crossed the great hall. He had a sword in his hand and was only wearing a kilt. Sweat sheened all over his heavily muscled chest.

Damn, are there any normal-sized guys here?

The man on his heels was wearing pants but was also missing a shirt. The sword at his waist was sheathed. He looked *just* like the guy in front of him.

Twins?

"Duncan!" Claire's shout made her jump. "Duncan, my sister is here!"

"So, Cormac said. But how, *mò gradh*?" the kilted one spoke, sheathing his huge sword.

Her sister's husband kissed Claire and swept the toddler into his arms.

The tiny boy giggled and clutched his dad, throwing small arms around his thick neck.

Then her sister slid her arm around the guy's waist and grinned.

Jules' heart stuttered.

Her sister glowed with love. She had a child with the man at her side. How was she going to get her to come home?

"Hello, I'm Alex, Laird of Clan MacLeod. Are ye well, lass? Ye look pale."

"I-I'm good." Jules met concerned blue eyes and forced a smile. "Happy to be with my sister again."

Alex smiled and squeezed her hand. "Welcome, lass. Yer family as much as Claire is."

She took a breath—because she kind of wanted to fall over—and nodded. "Thank you."

The guy was hot, but his eyes were kind.

"Our cousin said ye arrived with a MacDonald?"

The name was a curse, and Claire's husband scowled as he spoke.

"Yes, the laird, Hugh, found me on the beach."

"Did he hurt ye?" This was a demand from Alex.

Jules squared her shoulders. "No."

Duncan studied her. "Did tha' coward wretch put his hands on ye?" His voice was low, full of menace.

Jules prickled. Wanted to defend Hugh for some reason.

Seriously?

He manhandled you. Kissed you. Touched you.

Kidnapped *you.*

You want to defend him?

There you go again, Stockholm-Syndrome-Girl.

"He-he-he didn't hurt me." Jules forced the words out and swallowed. Shifted in the borrowed boots.

Nice going. Stuttering? Again?

Now she had her sister's keen interest. Claire stared; fair eyebrow arched. "Duncan, Alex, I'm going to take Jules up to the solar. We need to talk. Alone."

Jules could have kissed her sister.

Claire stood tiptoed to press her lips to the kilted man's mouth and took their child back into her arms.

"I'll have Mairi bring some food," Alex said.

"I'm not hungry, but thank you," Jules blurted.

"Verra well, if ye are, please let Claire know," the laird said.

Jules nodded.

"Go back to the yard and your sparring. We're fine

here. I want to talk to my sister before the family descends." Claire smiled.

The men headed out of the great hall.

Claire took Jules' hand. "C'mon. Let's go to the solar."

"Solar?"

"It's a sitting room with lotsa windows that hold the warmth. I spend a lot of time there with Alana, Alex's wife, and Janet, Duncan and Alex's sister. *My* sisters now."

Jules ignored how the comment had bite.

Claire wasn't trying to hurt her feelings; she was just stating a fact. Both women were her sisters-in-law. Her tone said she cared for them, too.

"What, have you learned how to knit or some shit?" she teased instead.

Claire — like her — had always been a tomboy.

"Yeah, there's no TV here." Her sister threw her a look that was half-amusement and half-annoyance. "It's called needlework."

She snorted. "Big difference."

Claire flashed a grin. "I'm so glad to see you."

"Yeah, me too."

They climbed a wide staircase and went all the way down a long, dark corridor.

Claire pushed open the room at the end of the hall, and light exploded, making Jules squint.

"See? The solar. Sunny. Warm. Comfy." Her sister pointed to the various chairs and sofas. There was a fire lit in the wide hearth, the scent of peat moss filling the air.

Claire set the baby down on a piece of tartan on the floor not far from the hearth. It was a different pattern than the dark red of MacDonald. She assumed it was MacLeod, since it matched the kilted guards at the gate, as well as what her sister's husband had been wearing.

Lachlan cooed and waved a wooden block around, babbling happily. There were several more in front of him, along with a stuffed doll. The figure was a boy, clad in a kilt with the same plaid he was sitting on.

Jules grabbed her sister's arm as soon as the door was shut. "Claire, I want you to come back home with me. Back to the twenty-first century. Back to Texas. Bring your son and come with me."

"No."

"Claire—"

"I would never take my son away from Duncan. Nor would I leave my husband." Her sister's green eyes flashed, and she propped her hands on her hips. "I haven't seen you in almost three years, and I don't want to argue with you." Her words had a slightly Scottish edge, but Jules didn't focus on that.

"Three years? I saw you last week."

"Maybe in your time, but I've been here two and a half years, Jules."

Your time.

The words rocked Jules to her soul. "Claire." She rested her hands on her sister's shoulders. "Think about Lachlan. Modern day meds, computers. Hell, even TV. He'll never know any of that here."

"I *am* thinking about him. How could being raised with technology be better than being with his father?"

Jules frowned. She didn't have the balls to retort to that. They'd been raised without either parent, so she didn't blame her sister for wanting her kid to have both.

Foster care sucked.

Her sister's eyes were kind, not angry, when she met her gaze. "I made a choice. I chose Duncan and the past. My life is here. Duncan and Lachlan *are* my life.

Jules bit down until her teeth ached and her jaw creaked. "I can't lose you, little sister."

"I don't want to lose you, either. But I'm happy here, Jules. I promise."

"Without...*everything* you know?"

Claire laughed. "I do miss tampons."

Jules swallowed a giggle. "But not antibiotics?"

Her sister scrunched up her nose, reminding Jules of when they were little. "An epidural woulda been nice."

"I bet." She snorted.

Claire took a chair and planted it next to her son. She motioned for Jules to join them. "You can always visit, you know. Magic is real and all that."

Jules rolled her eyes but couldn't stop smiling when she sat on the tartan and Lachlan toddled over to her. "I have a feeling this is a one-time trip. Not a fan of the disorientation. Oh, and the naked part." She took the baby's hand when he reached for her.

Claire grinned down and patted her shoulder. "I bet Laird Hugh MacDonald liked that part."

She stilled, avoiding her sister's gaze as her neck burned.

"I thought so."

"*Thought so?* What does that mean?" Jules bristled and scowled.

"Juliette Ann McGowan. You. Like. Him." Her only sibling sounded so damn smug.

Jules glared. "He's a freakin' barbarian. Like a real one. Like him? I think not. Wait 'til I tell you what he did to me. *Kidnapped* me. Carried me around like a sack of potatoes." She bit her tongue on the kissing and touching — and sharing a bed. Claire would have a field day.

"You were *pissed* when the twins were talking crap about him. You shoulda seen the look on your face. I can still read you like a book, big sister."

"Was not."

Claire threw her head back and laughed. "Methinks the lady doth protest too much."

"How seventeenth century of you," Jules snapped, which made her sister fall into a fit of giggles.

Lachlan laughed too and climbed onto her lap.

She distracted herself with an armful of adorable baby, but she managed another glare for his mother.

"I think..." Claire's chest heaved as she tried to catch her breath, "that Shakespeare said that, so it's more like sixteenth century."

"Shut up."

Her sister slipped off the chair, kneeling on the tartan and threw her arms around Jules. "God, I missed you."

"I missed you, too." Jules stroked her sister's long hair, sighing against her.

Lachlan hugged them both with his little arms and they laughed when their eyes met.

"He likes you," Claire said. She ran her hand through her son's curls.

"Of course, I'm awesome. I'm gonna be his favorite aunt."

Her sister smirked, but then her expression sobered. "I cried the day he was born. I thought you'd never see him. I tried to stop, but I couldn't. I made Duncan feel like crap." Claire's green eyes went misty, and Jules kissed her cheek.

"Well, I've seen him now, and he's gorgeous." She stroked her nephew's dark curls and he smiled, patting her cheek, and babbling. She grabbed his little hand and blew raspberries on his palm.

Lachlan giggled and clapped.

Claire grinned. "Thanks. I think so too, but I'm his mom, so I'm biased."

"His dad isn't so bad either." Jules smirked.

Her sister's gaze held a wicked glint. "No, he's not. He's *hot*."

Jules laughed. She refused to think about Hugh as

he popped into her head. He was hot, too. "You're really happy here, Claire?" she whispered, scrambling for anything but the MacDonald laird.

"Yes." Her sister's nod was earnest, but she flashed another grin. "Or, *aye*, I should say."

She found herself smiling again. Claire was practically radiating happiness. Jules knew her sister too well to think any of it was for her benefit. She sighed and averted her gaze.

Going home without Claire didn't sit right in her gut. Even if Jules could see with her own eyes how happy she was. "You found *happily ever after,*" she muttered.

"I did," Claire whispered. "I really did. I love Duncan and Lachlan more than life itself. I love his family. You'll meet them soon, I'm sure. Janet's pregnant and about to pop, so she's resting, but she's fab. Her husband is Fae, but so's Alana."

"Like Bree."

Claire stilled. "Bree?"

"The chick that helped me get here. Opened the…Faery Stones?"

Her sister nodded. "Yeah. The Faery Stones." Claire's eyes were narrowed, and she cocked her head to one side.

"Something wrong?"

"I don't know. Where'd you meet this chick?"

"I put an ad in the paper when you went missing. She saw your pic and answered it."

"What?"

Jules' instincts pricked and she sat straighter, letting Lachlan go when he pulled away. "Claire, what's wrong?"

"Keep talking, Jules. What else happened?"

"She said she was from here. Like this century, and she knew you. She said she could help me get here because she needed to go home."

Claire's green eyes were like saucers. "Bree? You said her name was Bree?"

She nodded. "Yeah. When Hugh found me, I couldn't find her; I looked."

"What did she look like?"

"Why?" Alarm shot down her spine and she sat taller on the tartan. Her police instincts switched to the *on* position.

Her sister's chest rose and fell with a breath. "Just...tell me." Claire was leaning into the edge of the chair's seat, gnawing on her lower lip. She'd propped herself up in it again, as if she couldn't sit still.

Jules frowned. "She was about your height. Shorter than me. Long dark hair. Brown eyes and darker complexion, like she was Hispanic or something. But she's Irish. Said her grandma was Fae. I didn't believe it until the bubble thing opened."

Claire gasped. "Bridei."

They both ignored Lachlan tugging on his mom's sleeve.

"What?"

"Her real name is Bridei. She's dark-skinned because she's a gypsy. We thought she was dead."

chapter ten

Jules could only stare as Claire explained a ton of unbelievable things—despite the fact she'd time traveled. People with wings called Fae Warriors. Magic. Funky colored trees and grass in a place called the Fae Realm.

Evidently her *friend* Bree wasn't exactly good people.

Claire's husband cursed savagely. It wasn't English, but there is no doubt he was, in fact, swearing up a storm.

The whole freaking family—including the pregnant chick—had filed into the solar.

"What's the problem?" Jules asked. "She didn't seem bent on some revenge plot or anything, she just wanted to get home."

"You don't understand, lass." A guy with purple eyes—like for real violet purple—spoke. He had white-blond hair and was as freaking tall—and built—as the MacLeod twins.

He was also so good looking it was almost unnatural. Claire had told her he was a former Fae Warrior, but Jules didn't see any wings. Maybe he removed them?

"What don't I understand?"

Alana, who was supposedly a *real* princess, stepped forward. She was beautiful—ethereally so. Long, white-blonde hair was loose to her waist, and she wore a shimmery lilac gown. Her eyes were purple, too. She looked related to the former Fae Warrior, but no one had said so. "Bridei's lover was killed when we were fleeing."

Ah, so that's what Bree left unsaid.

Jules remembered the emotions flashing in the woman's dark eyes. "Well, she's disappeared now."

"I dinnae believe she'll remain so," Alex said.

Duncan nodded from beside his brother. Both twins had shirts on now, but their stances were the same—crossed arms over broad chests. Alex had donned a kilt, so they looked even more alike. Swords were sheathed at their waists, too.

"Her magic isn't that strong here, so I guess we have that going for us," Claire whispered.

"Time may have changed that, I'm afraid," Alana said. "We just cannae know."

Claire nodded, a frown marring her face.

Jules sighed. Maybe she shouldn't have readily agreed to go with Bree. Then again, she wouldn't be sitting here, having this conversation, nor would she know Claire was okay, had she not. Or have met her adorable little nephew. She made a fist and shook her head.

"Jules, don't worry. You didn't know. Besides, she

brought you to me. For that, I'm grateful." Her sister hugged her, and Jules squeezed her tight.

The twins exchanged a look over Claire's head that Jules didn't miss.

What's the real danger they're not mentioning?

"We must find her," the purple-eyed guy said.

"I agree, Xander." The laird spoke, his mouth a hard line. He looked at his brother. "We need ta send the men out. Small groups. Scour the Isle."

"Jules can help!" Claire piped in.

All the men in the room zoned in on her sister, but no one said anything.

"Jules is a cop—a police detective," Claire continued. "You remember me explaining it to you, Duncan? It's like…a knight."

Now both twins, and their father had dark brows drawn tight, but the silver-haired guy looked thoughtful.

"I catch bad guys for a living. Criminals. Law breakers." Jules nodded. She waited for the tell-tale *but you're a woman*, which was sometimes even present in the twenty-first century.

"Verra well." Alex cocked his head to one side. "Do ye remember where ye saw Bridei last?"

"Well, not specifically. I was pretty out of it when I came to on the beach, but I'd be happy to help." Besides, it would give her something to do. Maybe even wipe Hugh MacDonald from her head.

A giggle floated into the room, and a baby girl

popped in from thin air — literally. Jules blinked to clear her vision — surely, she'd just lost it — but a dark-haired child had most definitely just joined them.

Alex lifted his arms to catch her, gathering the baby to his chest.

Good thing because she didn't look old enough to walk. Which just made the situation even weirder.

"Alexandria." Alana frowned. The name was an admonition, but as beautiful as the baby.

"Well, if the clan dinnae believe in the Fae before, they're certain ta now." Duncan shook his head, but his words were wrapped in amusement.

"Umm…." Jules rubbed her eyes.

Nope. Kid's still here.

"My daughter can *blink*." Alana's voice was a breathy sigh.

Claire giggled. "Lately she does it a lot. Lexi, come here!" Her sister opened her arms and the baby disappeared. Only to appear seconds later in Claire's embrace.

Jules frowned. "What the hell?"

"*Blinking* is a magic ability." Xander finally put Jules out of her misery. He pressed his very pregnant wife, Janet, into a chair and rubbed her shoulders as he spoke, even though the brunette beauty had told him not to fuss over her. "Alana and Angus can do it, too. They picture where they want to go in their minds," he tapped his forehead, "and simply appear there."

"So like travel by telekinesis?"

"Aye, teleporting," Claire answered. Everyone else looked confused by the words Jules and her sister had said.

"Yeah, that's the word I was looking for. Wow."

"Pretty much." Claire bounced the cute kid in her arms.

"She's too young to understand magic in the castle can be dangerous, despite my attempts to explain." Alana's fair brows drew tight.

"It's just natural for her." Claire smiled at her niece.

The baby reached for Claire's face, patting her cheek, and giggled. She had dark hair, like Duncan and Alex, but her eyes were big and violet, like Alana's. She was beautiful, with chubby pink cheeks and the most perfect rosebud mouth that'd make a vain woman jealous because of the natural red color.

"When she's mad at Alana, she always finds her dad." Claire's green eyes danced.

The princess frowned. "My daughter and I will have words, no doubt, many times as she grows."

Alex chuckled and kissed his wife. "Dinnae fash, *mò chridhe,* I'll always be here ta intervene."

"Or gather wagers." Duncan smirked.

Claire giggled and Jules had to swallow to school her expression.

The princess didn't look pleased with her man and his brother—or Claire. Alana's gorgeous face was twisted in a scowl.

Xander cleared his throat to cover what suspiciously sounded like a laugh and Janet was grinning, too.

The patriarch—his name was Iain—sat in a chair by the door, beaming and shaking his head.

Jules watched the dynamic of the people in the room and her stomach flipped. They were her sister's *family*. Didn't matter that they were four hundred years removed from what was familiar.

People were the same here.

Touches and smiles were the same.

Love was the same.

She bit down to stave off unwanted emotion.

Jules was going to lose her sister.

At least Claire belongs here.

For some reason, Hugh danced into her head. Her heart sped up, but she ignored it. She wasn't where *she* belonged. Not in Scotland, and definitely not in 1675. Dwelling on the MacDonald laird was more than foolish—something Jules never allowed herself to be.

Claire handed the baby over to her mother.

The movement caught Jules' eye and her gaze collided with her sister's, tugging her from her thoughts.

"You okay, big sister?"

"You got it." Jules plastered on a smile.

Claire came to her side and slipped an arm around her waist. She squeezed in comfort, as if she'd known Jules was full of crap.

She was far from okay. Didn't feel like being specific. "When do we start looking for this chick?"

"Now," Duncan said.

Jules had everyone's full attention when she explained Bree—Bridei, whatever—had been *living* in the cave of the Faery Stones in the twenty-first century.

No one expected her to be stupid enough to stick around in *this* century, but all the men agreed it would make sense to start there.

Jules and Bree had arrived in 1675 via the portal, after all.

It didn't take long to get organized and mount up to head there.

Duncan felt they needed to start before it got dark, and the Fae halfling—as they all called her—had had a head start, because Jules had been with Hugh at Armadale all day and overnight.

She rode her own horse and couldn't help looking over her shoulder for a big black stallion, chiding herself every time.

The beach didn't even look remotely familiar, although it couldn't be far from where Hugh had found her. She'd been naked and disoriented, so Jules didn't figure she could've wandered far.

"I don't think I was this far down," she said to no one in particular. She glanced around, sitting taller on the dark brown pony Duncan had given her to ride. He'd told her the beast was gentle and would be easy for an inexperienced rider.

"Alana has magic covering the area, so I wouldn't expect you to remember where you were." Xander's smile was kind as their eyes met.

She was struck silent for a few heartbeats. The guy really was almost *too* good-looking. No man should have eyes that color or cheekbones that high. His face was flawless. Hairless and supermodelesque. His short white-blond locks shifted in the breeze as Jules maintained eye-contact with those violet orbs. "Ah."

Xander smirked. "Lass, I can read your thoughts."

Heat kissed her cheeks. "Uh, sorry." She averted her gaze and took a breath. Jules was kind of glad he didn't give her an opinion on her thoughts about him.

"Don't fash. Just picture a wall in your mind. It will help."

She looked back at the Fae man and nodded. "Thanks for the tip. But if you can read my mind, can you read everyone's?"

"Aye. Except my wife's."

Well, that's irony if I ever heard it.

"Geesh. That sucks. Sounds like it'd be noisy. How do you get any peace?"

Xander smiled again, this time his feelings for his wife palpable, making him practically glow. "Janet gives me peace."

Envy roiled Jules' gut, but she ignored Hugh's face

when it popped into her head.

The look he sported suggested he'd caught that as well, and Jules frowned.

She consciously constructed a version of The Great Wall in her mind and screamed at herself to stop thinking of her barbarian.

"Jules, grab the reins tighter. Garron will wander."

She jolted at her sister's admonition, but straightened and forced another nod. Jules muttered thanks and bit back a jibe to Claire that went something like, *'since when are you a master horseman?'*

Her sister rode a white filly that was slender and gorgeous. She'd told Jules her name was Fancy, and she definitely looked it. The horse was larger than the long-haired Highland pony Jules sat atop.

They might be Texans by birth, but both were most certainly city girls. Neither had been on horseback, save a petting zoo pony ride or two when they'd been little. They'd had one or two foster placements that'd been decent and 'parents' that'd taken them to an occasional carnival.

Xander's gaze was warm, concerned, when their eyes met a second time, but Jules didn't say anything to the former Fae Warrior about what he'd most likely 'overheard.' "We're close to the cave."

"Good." Jules shifted on Garron's back and wrapped the leather reins tight around her knuckles. "I don't think Bree will be there. She was pretty insistent on getting home."

"I dinnae disagree, lass, but 'tis worth a look." Duncan sat on a huge white stallion and nodded as he maneuvered around her and Xander to the front of their group.

Jules' stomach lurched and a sense of dread washed over her. "I don't feel so good." She swallowed hard—twice—to talk the 'ol tummy out of tossing her breakfast. Was the horseback ride making her nauseous?

Riding with Hugh hadn't bothered her.

Stop saying his name!

"Magic. I think I feel it, too," Claire said.

"Alana's spell is designed to make being in the area undesirable," Xander said.

"Well, it works," Jules forced out.

Duncan called a halt, one arm up, and they all dismounted.

Jules bounced on her heels when her boots hit the sand, but she was glad she didn't face-plant since her legs wobbled and her ass ached from the ride.

Her sister grabbed her arm and flashed a smile. Claire had put on some pants, but she'd had to argue with her husband to be able to tag along.

Men.

No, not just men. *Pushy Highlanders.*

Alana had stayed with Janet and the kids, but Alex had allowed his son, Angus, to come. The kid had proudly announced to Jules he'd just turned twelve.

He was basically a mini-Alex, with shaggy dark

hair and blue eyes. Tall for his age, too, so no doubt he'd be a giant like the other men in his family when he was done growing.

Jules almost wanted to ask what was in the water. All the MacLeods she'd met were broad and tall. Muscled from hard work, even the shortest of the bunch still had to stand about six feet. The women were on the tall side, too.

Xander said some words she didn't understand.

The pressure and trepidation melted from her body. She felt lighter and rolled her shoulders. Jules heard many of their group—which numbered about twelve not including the Fae man and the twins—whispering sounds of relief and straightening their backs.

Duncan's cousin Cormac winked when Jules met his gaze. He was cute, in a rough way. Sporting a short beard, he had pleasant dark eyes—that were nothing like a certain barbarian's even though they shared a color.

Dammit Jules, really?

Duncan's shouted orders to spread out yanked her from her thoughts. The men jogged or rode away, and Cormac—who was their best tracker, according to Claire—got down to business on the beach.

Jules followed her sister when Alex motioned the remaining group forward.

She looked around. Foggy recognition kissed her mind. The area looked like itself in her century, but the cliff was wider, more defined. Sat further from the water, too. The fissure that doubled as an entrance to the cave containing the portal wasn't significantly different, either. Wider, maybe. Except the big MacLeods in front had to turn sideways to enter.

"Nothin'," Claire announced when they'd all piled inside.

Xander hovered with a torch over Jules' shoulder as she turned her cop brain on and started to look around. He'd probably read her thoughts again, and he knew what she was trying to do, but she wasn't complaining. She needed the light to mentally catalogue everything around her.

She circled the Faery Stones—which pretty much looked the same in modern times. The center crystal that sat higher than the rest caught the firelight and seemed to wink at her. "I don't see any signs that *anyone* was here," Jules said.

"I sense Alana's spells and the normal hum of the Stones," Xander said.

The twins and Claire exchanged a look but said nothing.

Angus stood next to his father, much too quiet for a kid his age. Deep concentration overtook his expression. "I feel nothin', Da," he said after a few moments. "Nay other magic, Xander."

The Fae man nodded, and Alex patted the kid's shoulder, muttering something in Gaelic.

Claire had told her Angus was like his mom, had

a lot of magic.

"If she wanted to go to Ireland, how could she get there?" Jules asked.

"The lass could hire a ship," Xander said.

"With what money? And no clothes. If I was naked, so was she."

Xander gave her a long look, and Duncan smirked.

"Tha lass needs nary a coin. Desperation guides her," Alex said. His eyes darted to his son, as if the boy's presence was keeping him from being frank.

"But how would she..." Jules looked at Claire, who wore an uncomfortable expression. "Oh..."

A little slow on the uptake there, Jules.

Bree would sleep her way onto a ship?

Eww.

"We dinnae ken where she may go," Alex said, his head tilted to one side.

"All I know is she was very insistent on getting home."

"For all *we* know, she went into the Fae Realm," Claire remarked.

The men seemed to consider that for a few moments of silence.

"We dinnae ken," Duncan said finally, slipping his arm around Claire's shoulders. "But if tha lass is on Skye, we dinnae cease 'til we find her."

They searched the beach and surrounding hills until it was dark. Cormac confirmed the only trail he'd scented out was a faint one that was probably Hugh's horse, but there were no signs of Bree or anything else.

"She may have masked her trail with magic, though I sense nothing," Xander said when they'd all remounted their horses.

"Nay, I dinnae feel anathin'." Angus nodded emphatically. "*Mamaidh* said she would know if tha Stones opened, and they dinnae. I too can feel them. They call ta me, bu' now they sleep."

"Good job, lad."

The boy beamed at his father's praise and sat taller on his Highland pony.

The ride back to Dunvegan was full of strategy and observation. Duncan had two shifts of men he was planning on sending out to scour the island, and three of his cousins agreed to stay out overnight—or at least longer than the rest of them.

Jules quickly explained how she would set up a search grid and was shocked that her sister's husband and his brother not only listened but took her suggestions to heart.

At least Duncan and Alex aren't barbarians.

She smirked, then screamed at herself for the hundredth thought of *him*.

You're freakin' hopeless.

Claire showed her to a guest room as soon as they were sealed safely inside Dunvegan's walls, and Jules soaked in the wooden tub when her sister insisted, she needed a bath. It was probably a good idea after the horseback ride. She didn't need stiff muscles in the morning.

When she climbed into the big, borrowed bed and lay down, all Jules could see was Hugh MacDonald when she closed her eyes—no matter the amount of cursing at herself.

She couldn't help but wish he was next to her.

Dammit.

chapter eleven

ife seventeenth century style started *early*, and Jules yawned her way through breakfast and mourned the *no-coffee* thing.

She should be used to it, since it was the third morning she'd woken up at Dunvegan, but not so much.

Duncan had offered her mead, but she certainly wasn't going to drink an alcoholic beverage before noon. The warm milk option was out, too. She hadn't had a glass of milk since she was a kid. Besides, it was goat's milk. Just…ew.

"Awfully picky, big sister, arencha?" Claire winked and sipped water—the only option Jules thought about going for.

"Scots eat weird stuff in the morning. Even in the future."

Her sister laughed when all the males at the table grumbled.

Jules pretended to not notice and reached for a warm roll—the only offering that looked appealing.

Claire handed her a small pot of honey and she muttered thanks as she poured some on.

The bread was moist and warm, the honey sweet

on her tongue. Jules sighed and closed her eyes. She fidgeted in the stupid corset that was stealing her breath. Day three wasn't working for her attire, either.

"You don't want your boobs on your stomach, do you? No bra, get used to it," her little sister had said the first morning, when she'd popped into her guestroom with clothes.

The corset was tight and did the job of supporting her breasts, but damn. It was *uncomfortable.* And way too girly. All feminine curves and the fabric had a sheen even though it was black. Every night when she'd taken it off, her torso had ached, no matter how long she'd lingered in a hot bath.

The shirt Claire had given her—she'd called it a leine—was ivory and had puffy sleeves, but Jules didn't mind that. The neckline was low cut and didn't constrict.

She'd refused a skirt and Claire had rolled her eyes but had given her a pair of pants that actually fit—unlike the ones Mab had found. They were dark brown brushed leather, and as comfy as a pair of pj's. She didn't mind wearing them for the third day in a row.

The boots were the best part of her outfit. Deerskin, with fluffy insides and white rabbit fur at the top. They fit perfectly, and even though her sister hadn't said, Jules suspected they belonged to Janet. The woman matched Jules in height and build—minus the pregnant part, of course.

Movement to her right drew her attention, and

Jules' gaze collided with Janet's sapphire one—as if the woman had known Jules was thinking of her.

Janet smiled and reclined in her chair, rubbing her distended tummy.

Xander leaned over, kissing his wife's cheek. "Are you well, *mò aingeal?*"

"I am." The smile for her husband was brilliant and they gazed at each other as if there was no one else at the table—or in the world.

Jules tried not to stare, or admit she was jealous. Not of Janet for Xander or anything, but because she didn't have a guy to look at her like that.

Geeze, get over yourself. Since when are you a sappy chick?

She definitely ignored the memory of the very vivid—erotic—dreams she'd had *every stupid night* she'd been there, starring a certain barbarian and a whole lotta *naked.*

Xander placed a wide palm on his wife's stomach, a dreamy smile curving his lips.

"He's kickin' somethin' fierce this mornin'." Janet grinned.

"I hope he joins us soon," Claire said, biting into an apple.

"Me too!" Angus grinned. "I want to meet him."

"I hope ye all will be jus' as happy, if *he* is a *she*," Janet said.

Xander chuckled and whispered something in his wife's ear that made her blush and beam.

"'Tis a lad," Angus said.

No one contradicted the boy, and Jules bit back the urge to ask if he knew from some sort of magic.

Conversation and bantering continued until the men all tapered off to start their collective days. They'd discussed finding Bree for the hundredth time and mentioned the party that had already left Dunvegan before dawn to continue the search.

Duncan said they'd stop to question the local clans that had active ports and ships, *again*. The same had yielded nothing the day before.

The trackers that'd stayed out that first night had come back empty-handed, no leads.

Three days later hasn't changed nothin'.

Jules still didn't get what the big deal was. Bree had said she wanted to go to Ireland. She hadn't gotten the feel for anything other than the chick's honest desire for home. As a cop, Jules was usually pretty good at reading people. If the Irish woman had had mal intent, she'd masked it well.

She sat like some sad third wheel—or more like seventh—when Xander, Duncan, and Alex kissed their wives enthusiastically before leaving the table.

Hugh's face wouldn't stop haunting her, no matter how much it pissed her off.

"C'mon, Jules." Claire tugged on her sleeve. "We got stuff to get done."

A few hours later, Jules could've collapsed on her feet. She'd seen it three times now, but it was no less exhausting. Claire's day-to-day was filled with household chores—even though the MacLeods had servants.

She'd helped her sister whack dust from two huge tapestries that normally hung in the great hall. Duncan and Alex had dragged them out to the courtyard and hung them so the women could work.

Jules had pictured Hugh's face with every loud *smack*, so the outlet of aggression was pretty awesome, even though it wore her out.

Next, she'd helped spread rushes on the floor of the great hall—Claire said they did that once a week—and it'd taken five women to cover the vast space quickly.

She'd watched Claire and Alana consult with the women heading to the market to buy food for the household—there were a lot of mouths to feed.

Evidently, they always sent at least two guards with them, but because their best soldiers were out searching for Bree, two younger guys met them in the kitchen. They were probably late teens, but still tall, broad MacLeods. The younger of the two had bright red hair and blushed every time his blue eyes met Jules' gaze.

Alana was the Lady of the Castle, since she was married to Alex, but Jules got the impression that she and Claire—and Janet for that matter—all ran the place together. It was eye-opening to see her sister in a take-charge position, and Jules' admiration of her shot up more. Seventeenth century or not, her baby sister had found her niche.

"I need a break," Jules confessed when she and Claire made their way back into the great hall.

Alana had forced Janet to rest and had fussed her upstairs about ten minutes before. The princess said the dark-haired beauty wouldn't get into bed unless she had an escort, so she'd gone with her.

"That's fine. I'm gonna run to check on Lan in the nursery. He and Lexi should be napping. Meet you in the solar?"

"Does that mean I can relax?"

"Sure, I'll teach you how to embroider." Claire's lips rippled as if she was fighting a smile. "Or we can talk about the Laird MacDonald. Again."

Jules smirked and chose to ignore her sister's dig about Hugh. "Well, you're wearing a skirt and you did housework all morning—for the third morning in a row. I figure that rounds out your domestication quite nicely, lil' sis."

"Not that I'd ever admit to the likes of you." Her sister winked when Jules laughed.

"You kinda just did."

"Yeah, yeah." Claire grinned.

"See ya in a bit."

Her sister nodded, lifted her skirts, and jogged up the stairs.

Jules leaned back for a full body stretch, pushing her arms so wide her muscles protested. She felt *good*.

Even the mention of her barbarian hadn't dampened her spirits. She and Claire had—*unfortunately*—discussed the man too many times over the last three days. Her sister had accused Jules of being obsessed with him.

Am. Not.

She'd never admitted to kissing him, but Claire's green gaze was too knowing. Her sister saw right through her.

Dammit.

"Are ye well, lass?" A now-familiar female asked.

"I am. Thanks for asking." Jules crossed the distance to the wide hearth, returning Mairi's smile.

"Verra glad ta see ye wit' Lady Claire."

She met a pair of kind brown eyes. "I'm glad to be here, too." The truth of her statement hit when the words exited her mouth. Despite how she'd gotten to 1675, Jules wouldn't trade the time with Claire and her new family for anything.

The older woman stirred the contents of a giant black kettle over the largest hearth. Jules didn't ask what it was.

They spoke for a while, then she said a polite goodbye and sprinted up the stairwell to join her sister in the solar. The room was bright and warm as usual, and Claire was alone inside.

Her sister leaned over a small table, pouring mead into three glasses.

There was a plate of bread and cheese there also,

and Jules' stomach growled. All the hard work had made her hungry. She hadn't seen her sister bring the food up, but she was glad it was there. She wouldn't complain, even though she'd never been a fan of eating chunks of cheese.

"Where's Alana?" Jules asked.

"With Janet still. Said she would come as soon as Janet falls asleep."

"Ah, good. What about the kiddos?"

"Mairi said they'd just fallen asleep." Claire smiled and looked up from her task, clay pitcher still in hand.

"Mairi?"

"Yeah, she was with the kids," her sister said.

"Do you have more than one Mairi?"

"No, why?"

"She couldn't be with the kids, then." Jules frowned.

Claire straightened. "What're you talking about?" She arched one fair eyebrow as if she thought Jules had lost her mind.

"I just saw her. I mean, I was just talking to her. She was still in the great hall when I came upstairs, stirring something in a big pot. I assumed she'd be a while. Sure seemed like she was in the middle of something."

It was her sister's turn to frown, and Claire cocked her head to one side, making her long hair shift. Her green eyes were confused. "What do you mean? She's in the nursery, with Lexi and Lachlan."

Jules frowned again, as alarm crept up from her gut. "She can't be in two places at once, little sister."

Something's wrong.

Claire dropped the pitcher. It shattered at their feet. Mead shot out all directions, but Jules didn't pay attention to the scent of fermented honey filling the air.

Alex appeared in the doorway of the solar, a screaming red-faced baby girl in his arms. He was shirtless and covered in sweat, like he'd come in from the bailey. "Have ye seen Alana?" he asked, trying to comfort his daughter.

"No," Jules said.

"Lachlan," Claire breathed.

"What?" the laird asked.

Her sister rushed past Alex, who was having no luck at all with Lexi.

"The nursery, Alex. Were you just in the nursery?" Jules demanded.

"Nay. Came in from outside. Duncan an' Xander did so as well. Why?"

"How did you get Lexi?"

"She *blinked* inta my arms."

Jules' heart plummeted to her stomach, and she just *knew*.

Claire had said her niece always found her dad when she was *upset*. Even the tiny kiddo knew. "Shit," Jules spat.

Alex arched a dark eyebrow, but moved out of her way so she could rush after Claire. The laird came too, but his daughter's cries didn't quiet as they went.

Claire was crumpled by Lachlan's empty cradle, tears streaming down her cheeks. There was no one else in the nursery. "He's gone."

Jules ran to her sister, enfolding her into a hug.

Alex cursed savagely, already hollering for his brother, father and Xander.

Jules was glad they hadn't gone out with any of the search parties. They'd all been sparring out in the bailey with the remaining men.

"Alex. Bridei took my son," Claire wailed.

The laird didn't contradict her.

Iain and Xander tore into the nursery, both wearing identical expressions of confusion.

Alana appeared next, and Lexi *blinked* from her father to her mother.

Seeing the magic again and knowing what it was didn't make Jules feel any better. Tremors chased each other down her spine and she held her sister against her, rubbing Claire's back.

Nothing she whispered comforted her sister.

How Claire was so sure the Irish woman was the reason her son was missing; Jules couldn't bring herself to question aloud.

Alex seemed to believe it without a doubt, too.

Jules hollered at herself to be a cop about all this, but she was too busy comforting her sister. That was her first priority. Finding her nephew would come next, *very soon*.

Duncan was last into the room, the demand to know what was going on stamped all over his face, although he hadn't spoken yet.

Claire tugged away from Jules and rushed to her husband. "Bridei took our baby! Duncan, she took him!"

Her sister's husband caught her up, plastering her to his broad chest. "How?"

His angry shout made Lexi cry louder, despite the fact Alana now held her daughter, and the baby had calmed a little.

"Magic," Jules breathed.

Xander nodded, brandishing a fist. "I agree, lass. It's all over the room."

"A masking spell." Alana frowned, rocking Lexi with more vigor.

"Is that how Claire thought she saw—and talked to—Mairi?" Jules asked.

"Aye, that would do it," Xander said.

Claire whimpered.

Duncan squeezed her in a tighter embrace, but Claire hadn't stopped crying any more than her niece.

Can Lexi feel the magic, too?

Angus spilled into the nursery. "*Màthair, Athair*! I had a vision."

All the adults froze.

The baby girl disappeared again, only to pop into her brother's arms. Damn good thing the kid looked ready for her. He held her in his arms, rocking her like their mother had.

Lexi stopped crying.

"Angus-lad, tell us," Xander urged.

"The halfling lass—she's runnin' on tha beach wit' my cousin."

"Rally the men. Mount up, now!" Alex barked.

"She's taking him into the Fae Realm," Alana breathed. She had her palm on her son's forearm.

She didn't say so, but Jules got the impression she could see—and feel—what the kid had.

"But why?" Claire wailed.

"My brethren killed her lover. They'll kill Lachlan, too. Bairn or not, he's human. They will sense him immediately." Xander said.

"No!" Her sister's scream was even more anguished.

Jules' heart thundered as she reached for police professionalism, trying to forget that the child missing was her nephew. Or that Xander had said the little guy's life was in danger. "I hate that eye-for-an-eye shit. Let's get this bitch."

If anyone was offended by her language, they didn't show it as they rushed from the room together.

chapter twelve

The wind rustled Dubh's mane and Hugh's loose hair alike as they sat high on the ridge. He should just go home. He had no business watching the MacLeod stronghold, even if he *was* on his own lands and too far away to see anything of consequence.

He couldn't look away, as if her honey locks would appear at any moment. She'd shake her head and glare at him with those beautiful green eyes.

What're you going to do, if so?

It'd been three days…the three longest days he could remember having to endure.

Hugh chided himself again and again. Still, he didn't head home.

His stallion hoofed the sandy grass at his feet, shifting his step and giving a low neigh.

"What is it, laddie?" Hugh asked. He patted Dubh's dark neck, whispering to him to calm. It was unlike his horse to be skittish.

Dubh tossed his neck, making his mane fly.

Hugh cocked his head to one side as the cool air carried a cry to his ears.

A bairn?

He leaned forward on Dubh's back, listening harder. The cry became louder, as if a wee one was coming toward him, and in obvious distress.

Hugh urged his horse to turn, nudging his stallion slowly forward. If a child was lost, he would see him or her shortly. There were not many places to hide, despite the hillside.

But whose child?

There were no homes nearby, and none of the MacDonalds that resided remotely close to where he was had one so young. He knew his people well, down to the last clansman.

Hugh heard a woman's voice before he saw her. Her inflection wasn't Scottish, but neither was it odd like his foundling's. She sounded as if she was trying to soothe the fussy bairn.

"Who goes there?" he called, hand on the hilt of his claymore. They were on *his* lands, after all.

The lass froze when she spotted him. She did indeed have a bairn in her arms, but the laddie was not a wee infant. He was propped on her hip, his dark hair a mess of curls.

When he noticed Hugh, the tiny boy squalled even louder, his young face red, tears running down his cheeks.

Hugh's spine prickled as the lass's dark eyes widened.

Something's wrong.

"My laird." She inclined her head and attempted

to bend at the waist, clutching the laddie closer.

The bairn yowled.

"Somethin' wrong with yer wee one?" Hugh straightened and forced his voice even.

She shook her head. "He's fussy s'all, this fine day." The lass whispered to the child and plastered on a fake smile for Hugh.

Irish.

The lass was Irish.

The bairn shook his little head and pushed away from the woman, howling even louder.

Hugh narrowed his eyes. "What's his name?"

She shifted on her feet, bouncing him up and down. "He's named fer his father."

She's lying.

His gut shouted it. Hugh swung his leg over Dubh's back and dismounted.

Her eyes went even wider, and she took a step backwards as he towered over her.

The wee one screamed louder, his chubby cheeks apple-red. When he struggled in the woman's arms, something fell at their feet.

Hugh looked down at the same time she gasped.

MacLeod plaid.

When their gazes collided, the Irishwoman whimpered.

"Who does tha bairn belong ta?"

"Mine. He is mine."

"Nay. Ye dinnae even know his name." Hugh

made a grab for her, but she scooted away. "Give the lad ta me, and I will return him ta the MacLeods. If ye leave now, I'll tell them I found 'im on the hillside."

The woman snarled. "He. Is. Mine."

Hugh rushed forward and the woman screamed. The bairn cried out, but he was able to get his hands on him. He pinned the lad to his chest, praying he wasn't hurting him.

The lass gave a yell of rage and threw something to the ground. A puff of black smoke filled the air.

He coughed, shielding the child's face against his chest, but the laddie coughed, too. Hugh was dizzy as the air started to clear, but planted his boots in the grass so he wouldn't fall over or drop the bairn.

The woman had disappeared.

"Magic?" Hugh whispered. He blinked to clear his vision, searching the perimeter, but couldn't locate the child-thief.

He sighed and met the lad's gaze.

Big blue eyes regarded him, tears streaking round cheeks, but he wasn't crying any longer. He clutched Hugh's leine with two tiny fists.

"Laddie? Are ye well?" An unmanly tremor shot down his spine.

What do I know about bairns?

This one didn't look old enough to speak, so the question was foolish at best.

Hugh wiped the tears from his face, and the child smiled. For some reason, Juliette flashed into his mind, but he ignored how his heart skipped.

"Let's get ye home."

He was just as much of a stranger as the woman had been—he'd bet his favorite sword she'd stolen him—yet the lad seemed content in his arms, as if he knew Hugh meant him no harm. He might have no love for the rival clan, but he'd never hurt a child. Even a MacLeod.

"Who do ye belong ta?" Hugh asked as he climbed onto Dubh's back, the lad nestled against his chest.

Both his rivals—Alex and Duncan MacLeod—were married, so he could belong to either one. Maybe their sister? She too was wed now.

Or perhaps another clansman all together. He had the look of a MacLeod, even without the scrap of plaid. Dark hair and sapphire eyes.

Somehow, his flawless little face reminded Hugh of Juliette. Perhaps her sister's son? If so, the wee one did belong to Duncan MacLeod after all.

The laddie cooed in Hugh's arms, giving life to words of nonsense, and he had to smile. He shook his head. He'd no use for bairns, but this one was bonnie.

Hugh frowned when memories of his wife—and what he'd lost—entered his mind. He fought the urge to crush his eyes shut and banished her name. Refused to think about the child they'd lost. What he would look like now.

The lad would be ten.

"Nay!"

His shout made the tiny child in his arms jump.

Blue eyes misted over, and he sucked on his bottom lip. Sniffled.

"Sorry, lad. Dinnae fash. I'm takin' ye home." He rubbed the child's back until he settled again, resting his head against Hugh's shoulder.

Unfamiliar tenderness unfolded from his gut and crept up. Hugh locked his jaw and fought emotions he had no use for.

Bairns are to be protected.

He gathered him closer, trying to ignore the warm little body against his chest. This wee one was not his own, never would be.

After losing his wife and their bairn, he'd never planned on another. Refused his father's demands to marry again and provide a MacDonald heir, up to the day his da had finally passed away. He'd made an empty promise to the man on his deathbed—that he would marry again.

Hugh would probably rot in hell for lying.

Sweet Brenna was certainly in heaven. Holding their child for eternity.

He startled on Dubh's back as her name floated into his mind.

Nay.

Do not think of her.

Or remember the fear in her brown eyes the night they'd married. Hugh had been as gentle with her as he could manage. He'd been a fumbling lad of twenty, and she a lass of only six and ten.

He'd only had one previous lover at the time, and she'd been innocent.

Consummation had been quick and awkward, and he'd been afraid to kiss her, although he had when she'd asked it of him.

She gotten with child that very night, and he'd barely touched her afterward. His da had been overjoyed that he'd done his duty so well, and an heir was already on the way.

Then…

Labor had come early. It had been too rough on Brenna.

Hugh closed his eyes as a shudder racked his frame. He never thought of her, as a rule.

The bairn in his arms stirred, blinking large innocent eyes up at him.

He screamed at himself to get it together and brushed the lad's dark hair from his forehead. "Let's hie to Dunvegan, laddie." Hugh was rewarded with a shy smile, as if the wee one had understood what he'd said.

"Halt!" The voice was a shout, and Hugh was greeted by two MacLeods, claymores drawn.

A man equal his height and breadth strode forward. His dark hair was slicked back, and gathered at the back of his neck in a long ponytail. He stopped in front of Dubh, sword poised to run them through. "What business have ye at Dunvegan, MacDonald?" he demanded.

"*Laird* MacDonald," Hugh barked.

"What do ye want?" the guard growled, paying no notice—or respect—to Hugh's title.

"I've found a lad wrapped in MacLeod plaid."

Immediately the man's demeanor changed. He sheathed his sword and came closer, inspecting the bairn pinned to Hugh's chest. "Where did ye find him?" His voice and expression were filled with relief.

"I'll speak ta yer laird."

The guard nodded without another word, motioning for his counterparts to open the outer gates.

Hugh inclined his head and nudged his stallion forward.

A fair-haired lass raised her skirts and hollered as Hugh rode into the MacLeod bailey.

She ran right to Dubh's side, tears streaming down her cheeks. "Lachlan!"

The lad turned as his name was called, looking down on the woman who had to be his mother. He reached for her, leaning away from Hugh's chest.

Duncan and Alex MacLeod dashed from the doors of Dunvegan, on her heels.

"Thank you, thank you!" the lass chanted. Green eyes locked onto his.

Hugh couldn't look away from their familiarity.

This lass had to be Juliette's sister, Claire.

Hugh nodded and handed the bairn down.

MacLeods surrounded him and his stallion.

Horses and riders littered the bailey. They'd been mounting a party — probably to search for the missing bairn.

So he hasn't been gone for very long. Good.

Hugh spotted the old laird, Iain, as well as a tall, silver-haired man amongst the sea of MacLeod plaid. Many swords were drawn, but the looks on most faces were relief.

They all knew he meant them no harm.

Hugh squared his shoulders and met Duncan MacLeod's gaze. "Looks like ye lost somethin'." His attempt at a little humor didn't dissipate the tension.

Duncan strode forward and embraced his wife. Kissed his son's head, before looking back at Hugh. "Thank ye fer bringin' my son home." His voice cracked.

Whatever Hugh's retort, seeing his enemy's humble sincerity made it dissolve. He accepted the man's gesture when Duncan reached out and squeezed his forearm.

He recalled all the tussles they'd gotten into as lads. Hugh had always held his own, despite being several summers junior to the MacLeod twins. Now as grown men, and probably for some time, they were equal in height and breath.

Alex, the current laird, inclined his head. "I echo my brother. Thank ye fer returnin' tha bairn."

"Where did you find him? Did you get Bridei?"

"Ah, so ye know who snatched him?" Hugh asked,

ignoring the child's mother, and meeting his father's eyes.

"Aye, the seer witch disguised herself with magic and stole my lad from his nursery." Duncan's mouth was set in a hard line.

"She used magic ta get away from me," Hugh confessed. "Threw somethin' ta the ground, then disappeared in a puff a' black smoke." His eyes swept the area before him. He told himself he wasn't looking for Juliette, but he was.

The MacLeods asked a few more questions he forced answers to, but he was distracted. Wanted to see his foundling.

His heart skipped when she crossed the bailey to them.

Juliette was wearing trews that fit—dark in color and hugging those shapely thighs. She wore a black bodice over a flowing ivory leine. It propped her breasts high and made his cock tingle. Light colored, fur topped deerskin boots went up to her calves.

Feminine. Gorgeous. Mine.

Although she was dressed as a lad, no one would mistake her for one with all those curves. Hugh swallowed a growl. He wished for skirts so no one could see her body.

Juliette was his.

"Hugh." She inclined her head when she reached her sister's side but didn't smile.

For some reason, it bothered him, despite his

internal sense of triumph that she'd addressed him so casually when she should have shown him the respect of his title.

She kissed the bairn's head and whispered to Duncan's wife. There were nods and low feminine voices that didn't carry. Another female joined them.

This one had white-blonde, almost silver locks. Long and flowing freely down her back. Her beauty was ethereal. He'd never seen a Fae before, but this woman had to be Fae. The laird's princess wife, no doubt, as rumor had it. However, Hugh only had eyes for his foundling.

"Juliette." Her name was out of his mouth before he could help himself. Hugh swallowed when those green eyes settled on him.

She came to his side as if beckoned, his heart beating in time with her every step.

He couldn't speak. His tongue was glued to the roof of his mouth.

"What?" Annoyance flashed across her beautiful face, and she propped both hands on her perfectly rounded hips.

Hugh tightened his thighs around Dubh's middle and leaned down as far as he could manage. He grabbed her by the waist and plucked her off the ground.

As soon as he was sure Juliette wouldn't fall off the horse, he kicked his stallion as hard as he could, urging Dubh around.

Hugh plastered his lass to his chest and leaned forward, hollering at Dubh to move even faster. They sailed through the gates, ignoring the shouting MacLeods.

He prayed the laird didn't call for archers.

chapter thirteen

▶▶ **S**eriously?" Jules struggled against Hugh's chest, but he held her tighter and nudged his horse even faster. "You have some nerve, Hugh MacDonald. Or some giant balls."

His chest rumbled with a laugh she felt, more than heard. The wind ripped it away as they rode over the hills.

"I had ta take ye. I have ta have ye."

She stilled in his grip. "What?"

"I've missed ye, lass."

Her stomach flipped and her mouth went dry. She'd missed him, too.

Wow. Just wow.

He kidnaps you again *and you like the fact he missed you?*

Jules growled and punched at his chest with tight fists. "Take me back. Duncan and Alex will come after you, even though you saved Lachlan." She would've thanked him for returning her nephew, had he not *kidnapped* her.

"I ken it."

"You're not scared?"

"They dinnae be willin' ta hurt ye."

"Right, but I can't say the same for you."

"Ye will tell them I mean ye no harm."

Jules laughed. "Wow. You really do have some huge balls. Why the *hell* would I tell them that? You *kidnapped* me. Again."

"We will speak at Armadale. Hold on ta me."

She wanted to tell him to go to hell, but she tingled. His heat seeped into her clothing. Her traitorous body remembered his muscles and wanted more. The rough ride had her ass bouncing against his thighs, but she was facing him this time. Could easily wrap herself around him.

Jules wasn't afraid in the least—which should have pissed her off. Excitement and arousal rode beneath the surface.

She wanted to kiss him again.

Hugh panted in her ear, as if he could read her mind—or body. "Lass—"

Jules bit her tongue to keep from answering, or blurting that she'd missed him. She'd rather taste blood than see satisfaction on his face that she was actually *glad* to see him.

Sorta.

She'd never admit she'd thought of little else the whole time she'd been at Dunvegan—especially since she'd been surrounded by three happy couples.

His huge stallion leapt over a small burn, and she screamed; couldn't help it, even though hooves soon connected with hard ground and their pace increased.

"I dinnae let ye fall, hold on ta me, Juliette." His deep voice was urgent but confident. A promise.

Her heart rebounded against her ribs, but Jules nodded and slipped her arms around Hugh. She had no choice. If she fell from his horse at this speed she'd get hurt. Or worse.

He held her tightly with one arm, the other working the reins. Hugh whispered something in what she now recognized as Gaelic, but the language was lost on her, despite Claire trying to teach her a few phrases. It had an almost lyrical quality, but Jules' tongue couldn't form the words with the right twist.

Her sister could now speak it fluently, but she'd told her it'd taken almost two years to learn, and sometimes she still stumbled over words.

They rode hard, the stallion's cantering stride eating up the distance like a racehorse, at a much faster speed than Jules had ridden with him before. Armadale loomed, but they were coming in very fast, so it was growing larger and larger with every second. It seemed like it took only half the time to get there, compared to the previous, reasonable pace.

Hugh shouted orders as soon as the gate came into view and kicked the horse even faster.

Jules crushed her eyes shut as the stallion made another jump. She buried her face against Hugh's shoulder. She'd never been an amusement park kind of girl, and this was worse than any roller coaster Claire had ever managed to talk her onto.

The gates opened slowly, but Hugh didn't slow their pace.

At. All.

She sucked in her breath and held it as they soared through what looked like a sliver in the parted wood. They made it through, coming to a halt so fast her body pitched backwards.

Hugh's, too, but he held onto her, and neither of them fell.

"Close the gates!" He said another phrase in Gaelic, gesturing with his free hand.

A shout went up on top of the wall closest to the oversized gates and Jules froze in Hugh's grip.

"Ye were pursued, my laird." Colin's chest heaved as he dashed toward them.

"Aye, as expected." Hugh handed her down to his cousin, and Jules didn't fight either man.

The last thing she needed was to land on her face in the dirt.

"Hello, my lady."

She forced a polite greeting to Colin—after all, he'd never been anything but kind to her.

"Expected, my laird?" another MacDonald asked, dark eyebrow arched, his sword in hand.

"MacLeods!" someone shouted from the wall.

"Get ready!" Hugh returned.

"My lady?" Colin asked, his blue eyes confused.

"Hugh didn't *ask* me to come back, Colin."

The dark-haired MacDonald tensed but nodded.

He drew his claymore.

"Up on the wall, now!" Hugh shouted. "Archers at tha ready! Dinnae shoot until I say!"

Fear skittered down her spine. "Hugh, no. Please." Jules had spent three days with the MacLeods. They were all good people. *Family.*

Her barbarian spared her a glance and grabbed her hand. "Up ta the wall fer us, too."

Jules shook her head. "I don't want anyone to get hurt—"

"Come wit' me, Juliette."

As if I have a choice.

Men dashed up a narrow stairwell that made her stomach flip. Swords were drawn, as well as arrows knocked.

Hugh all but pushed her forward.

Jules shivered as she stumbled up the first, then tripped up the second step.

He slipped an arm around her waist and lifted her to keep her from falling.

Her head spun, and she let him do most of the work to get them to the top of the embattlement.

Hugh didn't release her as they arrived, and Jules could already hear angry shouts from below.

A glance over the side told her Duncan, Alex, Xander, and a dozen MacLeods circled the closed gates of the MacDonald stronghold.

Her sister, too, was there, sitting in front of her husband on his large horse.

"Scoundrel!"

"Wretch!"

"Release my sister-by-marriage! Now!"

"I *told* you they would come after me." Jules regained a little composure and tried to yank away from Hugh.

He turned her to face him and grabbed her wrists.

His dark eyes burned, but she wasn't afraid as she glared up at him.

"Juliette McGowan is mine!" Hugh hollered, but he didn't look away from her.

His gaze devoured her, and she stood frozen in place, wishing he would touch her. Kiss her.

Jules cursed when her heart sped up. She couldn't even muster a retort or tell him to go to hell for claiming her like a piece of property.

She wanted him.

Why?

Anger roiled her gut, but she couldn't gather the muscles or brain power to yank her wrists out of his big hands, either.

He wasn't hurting her.

Against her will, Jules remembered the last time he'd kissed her. In his rooms on her one night at Armadale. Tremors chased each other down her spine.

"Jules!" This time it was Claire.

She jolted — and so did Hugh if his expression was any indication.

"Hugh, let me go."

He hesitated.

"Please, Hugh. Let me talk to them. I don't want *anyone* to get hurt."

Her barbarian's nod was barely perceptible, but his hands opened, and she slipped from his grip.

Jules went to the edge of the wall and leaned down.

Hugh stayed close; she could feel his body heat at her back.

"Claire! I'm fine!"

Her sister sat with Duncan on his huge white destrier, probably even bigger than Hugh's stallion.

Alex was beside him, and Xander beside the laird, both on mounts just as large. Alex's was white, like his brother's, and Xander's dark brown.

All three men wore glares Jules could make out even from the height.

"Claire-bear, I promise! I'm good."

Claire shook her head.

Jules leaned over a little more, so she could see her sister better.

Hugh's thick arm shot around her waist. "Careful, lass."

His words were right above her ear, and his warm breath caressed her cheek, making her shiver.

"I'm not gonna jump," she tried to snap, but her statement shook, which had everything to do with his proximity.

His chest at her back, warmth sinking through her

corset and tunic. Even his thighs cradling her ass made Jules want him more—and pissed her off.

However, she couldn't jerk away, or they *both* could fall over the wall.

"Unhand her, Hugh MacDonald," Alex shouted.

"He's not hurting me." Jules rolled her eyes at herself.

Really?

Why did you say that?

Scream, yell, stomp on his foot.

She didn't. Couldn't.

"Ye heard tha lass! I mean her no harm! Hie back to Dunvegan. Leave us be!" Hugh's words rumbled against her.

"Bollocks! Ye'll force yerself upon her," Alex called.

He won't have to.

Jules cringed and crushed her eyes shut. "I won't let him!" she threw the words out because she had to answer for herself. She didn't want to hear what Hugh's retort to the MacLeod laird might be.

"Let tha lass go, MacDonald." Duncan's order was hard.

"We'll give ye time ta do so with no harm. We dinnae storm yer gates," Alex promised.

"I dinnae let ye go, Juliette." Hugh pressed the words into her ear.

Jules shuddered and his embrace tightened.

He slipped his other arm around her, pinning her

back to his chest, lifting her boots from the stone beneath.

"If ye refuse ta release her, we will attack!" Duncan yelled.

"I've men an' weapons, MacLeod," Hugh called. "Ye dinnae win! Armadale is strong. Archers at the ready!"

A chill racked her frame, despite Hugh's body heat surrounding her. People—her sister's family—could get hurt.

Or killed.

Because of me.

No.

Jules couldn't allow it. She cleared her throat. "I want to stay here!"

Everyone froze, including Hugh.

What just came out of my mouth?

Are you crazy?

"Jules." Her sister was the first to speak. Claire's voice was calm and clear. "Are you sure about this?"

"I am."

I. Have. Seriously. Absolutely. Lost. It.

She couldn't be the cause of a war. A voice chided that it had nothing to do with Mab's concerns, or even the MacLeod threats, and had *everything* to do with the man holding her, but Jules ignored it.

Banished it.

I'm just buying some time—and peace—until I can escape.

Besides, her brother-in-law had bigger things to worry about. They had to find Bree. Even though Lachlan was home safe, the culprit was still out there.

Jules could find her way back to her sister's castle, no problem now. When Colin had taken her, she'd paid attention to the route. It would take her an inordinate amount of time on foot, unless she could steal a horse, but she'd get there.

"Laird MacDonald." This time, Claire called to Hugh.

"Aye, my lady?" he said, his deep voice loud and thick against Jules' back.

She was half-surprised he had the manners.

"You won't hurt my sister?"

"Nay, my lady."

"I have your word?" Claire's voice was just as hard as her husband's had been.

"Aye."

"Ye dinnae be able ta trust him!" Duncan protested.

"Duncan, he brought Lachlan home. He didn't hurt him. He won't hurt Jules, either." Claire's voice was low and insistent, but the wind carried her statement up to the battlement.

Her sister's husband snapped his mouth shut, but his glare didn't lessen.

"I'll be fine, guys! I'll see you soon. Find Bree!"

Hugh growled in her ear but didn't disagree verbally.

Even from the distance, Claire's green gaze bored into Jules. She couldn't look away. "Jules…"

"I'll be fine Claire-bear. You know I won't let him hurt me."

"I know. I'm not worried about that."

Jules couldn't ask what her sister *was* worried about. "Kiss Lachlan for me!"

"Leave, MacLeods! Ye heard tha lass, she stays wit' me!"

Jules wanted to glare at Hugh for the triumph in his voice.

"Lay one hand on her an' I'll run ye through," Duncan growled, his arm extended toward them.

"I dinnae have yer threats, MacLeod!" Hugh's shout rumbled against her.

"'Tis a promise, *MacDonald*." Hugh's name was a curse on Duncan's lips. "If *one* hair on her head 'tis harmed."

"It's okay, Duncan. I won't let him hurt me," Jules called.

"I dinnae harm ye," Hugh said low in her ear.

The warmth of his breath shimmied down her spine and she trembled. "I know, Hugh."

He grunted, but said nothing, and Jules tried not to get swept away in the feel of his body against hers.

She needed to hold onto her anger, not the lust clouding her stupid, *stupid*, brain.

"See you soon, big sister! Don't worry about Bridei, we'll get her!" Claire waved.

"I know you will!"

The MacLeod twins wore matching scowls as they turned their horses from Hugh's gate.

No one spoke as the party rode away, but Duncan kept glaring over his shoulder until there was no way he could see them anymore.

"Put me down, Hugh." She tried to bark an order, but it came out as if she was begging. She winced.

"Nay, lass. Now tha' I've ye back, I'll dinnae be lettin' ye go."

Jules shivered.

He hadn't said *ever*, but somehow, she still heard it.

chapter fourteen

hugh set Juliette to her feet when they came down the narrow staircase of the embattlement to the dirt ground of the bailey, and he could *feel* her glare.

No matter; she'd told her sister—and the MacLeods—she *wanted* to stay at Armadale.

With me.

Was it for the sake of peace alone?

Juliette whirled on him, hands on her shapely hips. "Stop looking at me like that. I'm a captive all over again, huh? 'Cept this time you're not trying to ransom me. What *do* you plan to do?" The fire in those emerald eyes made his cock twitch.

He stared. "I'll have ye as my own."

"The hell you will."

Hugh was acutely aware that his surrounding kinsmen, from soldiers to the blacksmith, even the lasses whacking dust out of rugs, were watching. They'd all stopped their tasks to stare, like they had the first time he'd brought her to Armadale.

Of course, after the excitement of an armed party of MacLeods and his shouted order to close the gates after riding in at top speed, his peoples' *normal day* was ruined, even if they'd mustered the energy to return to their duties as soon as Duncan and Alex had retreated.

Juliette's accent was odd, to be true, but she was shouting, and there would be no mystery to her ire from the bailey full of MacDonalds. No lass of his clan would dare talk to him as Juliette was.

Would his people think him weak for *allowing* it?

He'd never strike her—or any woman for that matter. Mab had taught him better than that, and after all, his people were long used to his aunt speaking her mind.

However, Hugh wanted to yank Juliette to him and claim those pouty lips, kiss the frown off her face, and smooth her furrowed brow. Put his tongue in her mouth so she would cease hollering. She was firing his blood. "Juliette—"

She threw her palms out and slid back when he approached. "Get away from me, *Laird* MacDonald. I like you even less than I did before if that's freakin' possible. I certainly don't *want* you." Juliette's voice became even louder as she lectured him on the injustice of her second kidnapping and what she called *blackmailing* her into staying with him.

A few of his male cousins snickered.

The lasses made no effort to hide their shock. Even his servant girls wore gapes.

Hugh marched forward, towering over her. "Inside. Now."

Juliette paused, scowling. "The commands are

already starting?"

"Please." He dropped his voice and growled. Hugh hoped no one had heard him, but when he averted his gaze and caught Colin's, his cousin had one dark eyebrow arched.

Juliette cocked her head to one side. "Why?"

"So, we can speak in private." Hugh sighed.

"Private?" She narrowed her eyes.

He wouldn't be thwarted anymore. He gripped her upper arm and started walking.

She wrenched free of his hold before they'd taken two steps. "Don't touch me!"

Hugh leaned down, his mouth mere inches above hers, and tried not to stare at her lips. He reached for the anger inching up from his gut with both hands. "Go. Inside."

Juliette huffed and glared right back, but she turned and started walking. She made tight fists and swung her arms at her sides, but her stride was stiff and jerky. Anger flowed off her tense body in waves.

However, it didn't keep Hugh's eyes from watching the sway of her hips or how the fabric of her trews hugged her thighs and the roundness of her perfect bottom. He stayed close behind her but kept his hands to himself—for now. His cock jumped with every forward step she made, especially when she started up the three steps that led to the main entrance of his home.

"Stop looking at my ass," Juliette barked.

Hugh halted in his tracks — couldn't help it. Threw his head back and laughed. His lass could read minds.

She *tsked* and threw a black look over her shoulder but didn't stop her journey into his castle. At least she was listening to him.

"Just so you know, I won't let you order me around all the time."

"Oh, aye?"

"Aye." Juliette mocked him, but he liked the way his word sounded leaving her lips. "*If* I stay here, it's as your *guest*, as Mab said last time. I'm not *yours*. And I'll leave when I damn well please."

Hugh grabbed her upper arm again and whirled her to face him as soon as they'd made it into the great hall. Rested his hands on her shoulders and chided himself not to stare at her breasts. They sat high in her corset, baring too much flesh not too be tempted. The ivory leine beneath it was wide necked, low cut, showing her collarbone. "Ye'll do as I say, guest or no'."

"I will not. Hugh, I'm not here forever. I'm going home. To the *future*. As soon as you promise to play nice with my sister's clan. They have bigger things to worry about than you right now."

His heart dropped to his stomach, but he tried to ignore the thought of losing her — permanently. This was just about having her, right? The rest mattered not. "The MacLeods have nothin' ta fear from me, or any MacDonald."

"Then let me go."

"Nay."

"Hugh—"

"I'll have ye, Juliette. I've thought a' nothin' else since ye left me."

A shiver racked her frame.

He felt it beneath his palms.

Juliette swallowed and Hugh restrained himself from kissing her.

"Then what?" she whispered.

He leaned down and brushed his lips against hers. When she didn't scoot away as expected, Hugh tugged her to him and took her mouth properly. He pinned her to his chest and forced her mouth open, but like before, she kissed him back.

Hugh slid his hands down the stiff material covering her back and kept going, cupping and squeezing her perfect bottom with both hands. He lifted her, rocking his pelvis into hers.

She yanked away all too soon, her scowl back in place. "No, Hugh." Juliette put her hand up. Her face was flushed, and she panted, her perfect breasts heaving in that corset. She might be denying him with words, but her body wasn't.

One look at her kiss-swollen lips made Hugh bite back a groan. He was already hard and aching. He had to have her. "We'll speak in my rooms." He pushed words out but had to clear his throat. His voice was thick, desire evident even to his own ears.

They'd do more than *speak*.

He just had to convince her.

Like he'd told her before, Hugh wouldn't take Juliette by force, but her shaking form said he wouldn't have to.

He grabbed her waist and hauled her close again, then swung her up over his shoulder without another word.

She yelped, hollered, and struggled, but she didn't try to kick or punch him like she had before.

Hugh hurried his step. He'd not want to gain his aunt's attention. As it was, he was lucky she hadn't stormed the bailey when the MacLeods had been at the gate.

Obviously, word hadn't traveled its usual speed at Armadale. He had no doubt Mab would pound his doors down when she heard Juliette was here, but Hugh would deal with it then.

Now is for Juliette.

"Put me down!"

He didn't follow her order until they were shut inside his quarters.

"You can't just pick me up and carry me off every time we disagree!" Juliette's exasperation leaked into more than her voice. She threw her arms wide and paced.

"Why no'?"

"Really?" She froze with that one word, a fair eyebrow arched.

His Juliette was gorgeous, and he enjoyed her

temper. He closed the distance between them and reached for her.

"No. Not again. Don't you *dare* put your hands on me." His little lass's glare could have slain him on the spot.

Hugh flashed a lazy grin and twirled one of her honey-colored locks around his finger. "Ye certainly liked my hands on ye a 'fore. Just now. In mine own great hall."

Juliette scowled. She put both hands to his chest and shoved.

He planted his booted feet and didn't move an inch.

Their gazes collided.

Her mouth parted and Hugh's cock twitched. His trek up the stairs with his lass over his shoulder had done nothing to alleviate the heavy ache in his groin. He swallowed a groan and tugged her to him.

Hugh dipped his head down, claiming her mouth and muffling her yelp.

Instead of fighting him, Juliette slipped her arms around his neck. She opened for him, whimpering as she kissed him back.

This is different from the kiss in the great hall.

It was more.

She was fully with him this time.

Triumph shot down his spine. He lifted her into his arms and kissed her harder, squeezing her rear end as she wrapped her legs around his waist. He damned her trews to hell and back. Had she been wearing skirts; he'd already have his hands on her bare flesh.

Juliette fired him in ways no other woman ever had. His cock was hard and pulsing, demanding freedom so he could slip inside her sweet body.

Hugh had missed her over the last three days. Thought of nothing but his foundling, his Juliette. Not to mention, doing this. "Jesu, lass," he breathed into her mouth.

She moaned and tilted her head back.

He answered her silent request and set a line of kisses on her neck, nipped her earlobe and she wiggled against him.

"Hugh," Juliette breathed.

Her body was wrapped around his, her softness hitting his hardness in all the right places. However, they had too many clothes on.

"I dinnae take ye by force, lass. But by God, I burn fer ye."

She whimpered.

Hugh kissed her again because he couldn't *not* plunder her sweetness. Their tongues dueled. Juliette was kissing him back just as fiercely as he pressed his lips to hers. He slanted his mouth over hers again and again. His limbs shook, but he held onto her as tightly as she was holding on to him.

He needed more.

So much more.

He slammed her against the wall. Breath rushed from her lungs, and she had to pant, but Jules didn't give a shit.

Denial denial denial.

It all slid out the window.

Her need — of *him* — smacked into her, combusting her from the inside out. She might not have admitted to *Hugh,* she wanted him, but her body was shouting it.

What the hell are you doing?

He kidnapped you again!

Jules shoved it all away and kissed him harder when he dipped his head down again. Maybe she didn't *really* give a shit about all that. She'd been thinking of him, ranting about him for three days — hell, obsessing about him as Claire had accused.

She *was* attracted to him.

Wanted him.

No. It's more than that.

Maybe it had been from the start.

Hugh groaned and pitched his hips into Jules' pelvis. He was already hard. She could feel him. Too bad they had clothes on.

He bit her bottom lip. The sting made her moan as he licked and sucked it away, devouring her as she explored his mouth and he plundered hers.

Jules tugged his hair and arched into his chest. They both made noises that were lost in the movement of their fused mouths.

His kiss was rough and relentless. Raw, just like Hugh—and left her needing more.

When he started to thrust, she whimpered. The cool stone at her back and the heat of his chest against her corset-covered breasts was not enough. "Hugh," Jules begged. "More." She ripped at his tunic. "No clothes."

He growled and nipped her neck, laying a line of hot kisses down to her collarbone that left her trembling in their wake.

Her insides quivered. She bit her bottom lip to stave off another whimper.

Hugh reared back, his gaze raking her face. His dark eyes bored into her. "Ye want this, lass? Wan' me?"

"Yes." A breathless moan. It was all she could manage.

He stepped back so fast she almost fell into a heap. Her legs shook and she leaned into the wall to stay upright.

"Undress." The order should've irked, but it only made her sex ache.

Jules licked her lips and kicked off her borrowed deerskin boots. She pushed the breeches Claire had given her from her hips. They landed on the stone floor soundlessly, and her sister's idea of home-sewn panties was next.

Tremors of anticipation shot down her spine when

she looked at her barbarian across the room. Hugh wore *naked* well, and she didn't know where to look first.

She'd already known his chest was beautiful with its sparse dark hair and defined lines. His shoulders were broad, and his waist was just the right amount of tapered. His ass was perfection and she wanted to grab it while he thrust deep inside her.

Jules whimpered as her eyes trailed his body.

His erection jutted in all its glory and his thighs were thick. Dark hair was sprinkled down to his ankles, and her hands itched to trace it, rub the firm muscles of his calves with her feet when they were entwined.

She couldn't wait to be up against all that.

He was gorgeous — and he was about to be hers.

"Ye dinnae be naked," he growled.

Her heart and stomach jumped at the same time. "I'm trying." The corset proved a challenge to her shaky fingers.

Hugh crossed the room in two strides, knocked her hands out of the way and finished the job himself. He tossed the stiff garment across the room as if it offended, and whipped her leine up and off before Jules could even appreciate the fact she could breathe freely again.

He made no secret of looking up and down her body and she tingled, as if he'd caressed her. His growl of appreciation made her melt, and Jules moaned.

His dark eyes zoned in on her face. They were

black with desire. His cheeks were flushed pink, and his lips swollen from hers. His long hair was mussed from her hands, and she couldn't wait to get her fingers there to mess it up even more.

Jules wanted him with an intensity that should've scared her.

She yelped when he lifted her over his shoulder, but she held on and let him carry her to his big bed. Again, her breath was stolen when he tossed her—actually *tossed*—her to the center of the MacDonald tartan blanket, but for the first time, she didn't give a damn he was manhandling her.

Hugh wasted no time following her down, covering her body and taking her mouth again. He dragged his hands down her breasts, leaving her nipples hard and aching. He continued downward as their tongues danced, teasing her stomach muscles, and rubbing her lower belly.

Jules gasped into his kiss when he dived between her legs, tugging on her clit and sliding his finger inside her without preamble.

"Wet. For me," he groaned.

She didn't get a chance to answer.

Hugh thrust his erection inside her, filling her with one hard stroke.

She threw her head back and called his name, clutching his thick shoulders with both hands. He was *perfect*, stretching her, making her burn for him to move.

Hugh kissed her throat and tipped his hips forward, pausing to give her a moment to adjust to him. "Tight. Lass, yer goin' ta kill me." His voice was strained and their eyes locked.

Her heart skipped. "It's been a while for me," Jules blurted. Heat burned her neck.

Why did you say that, idiot?

His dark gaze intensified, and Hugh squeezed her against his chest. "Mine." He growled the word into her mouth and plunged even deeper.

She whimpered and returned his kiss, wrapping her legs around his waist as he started to thrust in earnest.

He was rough, took her harder each time he propelled forward, and she loved every moment of it.

It was Hugh unbridled, no control, and *she* had done this to him.

Jules moved with him, under him, raking her nails down his shoulders, which only seemed to encourage him.

He groaned, going faster, but he kept kissing her, and she couldn't stop touching him. His back, his ass, kneading and squeezing as he drove in and out of her.

They were covered in sweat and panting but she didn't care.

Never wanted it to end.

Her body tightened and she crushed her eyes shut. Jules' inner thighs quivered. She threw her head back into his pillow and screamed his name as orgasm crashed over her. Her vision wavered and her head spun. It was hard and fast and stole her breath as pleasure shot over her body.

Hugh grunted and stilled, but he tugged against Jules' hold.

She was dazed as her hands and arms loosened and he straightened above her, pulling out of her body.

Confusion washed over her, clearing her head a bit, as she watched Hugh lean back, palm his erection, and close his eyes.

He pumped once. His release shot out, over his hands and onto her stomach.

Jules watched, half insulted, half relieved. Realization hit her that they'd just had sex without a condom, and her birth control pills were in the far future—and it'd been almost a week since she'd had one.

She should *thank* Hugh for not coming inside her.

So why did it prick a bit?

Are my feelings hurt?

Their gazes collided.

He said nothing as he left the bed. He came back with a scrap of linen, silent as he wiped her down. Hugh cleaned himself as well, then he returned to her, wrapping Jules in his arms and kissing her into oblivion, scattering whatever she might've said to him.

Languorous heat spread over her already boneless body, and she couldn't believe she had any more energy to feel *anything*, but she already wanted him again.

"Juliette." His voice was thick and quickened her heart all over. "Jus' like I ken ye'd be."

Jules met his eyes, feeling vulnerable, despite what they'd just done. "Hugh?" His name fell from her lips as a shaky whisper, and she cursed herself.

If Hugh noticed, she didn't read it in his eyes. Her lover caressed her cheek, his dark eyes boring into her.

Jules couldn't have looked away if she'd wanted to.

"Perfect, lass. Yer perfect."

Now she could read his expression. His face, his eyes, shouted the same word Hugh had growled earlier.

Mine.

For some reason, Jules couldn't find her voice to disagree.

chapter fifteen

She rolled over and bumped warm flesh. Jules blinked to clear her vision and shoved her thick hair from her eyes. Sex and sleep had made her natural waves a tangled mess. She winced as she tugged her fingers through it. If she couldn't find a hairbrush when they got up, the morning was going to be a bitch.

Hugh was lying on his side, the MacDonald plaid low, only covering half of his ass. One powerful thigh was exposed, but the good parts were covered.

Jules stared.

He was...beautiful. Looked almost harmless as he slept, too.

The dull ache between her legs told her otherwise, but Hugh hadn't hurt her.

On the contrary, he'd made her feel good. *Too good.* Better than any other man she'd been with.

Despite his roughness.

Her eyes trailed his stubble, and she remembered how the prickle on her neck and breasts had turned her on. His powerful chest rubbing hers as they'd moved together. She'd shattered in his arms. Twice.

Hugh had pulled out both times without a word.

She hadn't gotten the balls to ask him why, but her mind wandered back to her conversation with his aunt about his wife.

Brenna had died in childbirth. If Hugh still loved her, perhaps he didn't want to risk a child with someone else, ever. She ignored the little niggling voice that the method wasn't one hundred percent. As well as the other voice that *hated* he might still have feelings for a dead woman.

Jules was nuts to let either sentiment hurt her feelings, anyway. She had no birth control. Pulling out was a favor to her, really. She was going home. Pregnancy was the last kind of souvenir she needed.

Although it *was* kinda hot watching him come. His head thrown back, dark hair kissing his shoulders. His cheeks flushed red, and eyes closed. Whole body shaking.

She shuddered as memories made her body tingle. Her sex throbbed. She wanted him again.

Fully entrenched in Stockholm Syndrome now.

Just call me Patty. Then again, did she *screw her captor? I'm worse.*

How could she want this man, this unmannered barbarian, to *touch* her?

"Damn, look at him. How could I not?" Jules wanted to drag her hands over his muscles, trace his eight-pack and even suck his erection into her mouth.

She should be worried about finding Bree. However, since her nephew was home safe, she couldn't think of anything but the man whose bed she was in.

Hugh hadn't really let her explore his body. It seemed to be a mix of impatience and desire, but what if he didn't want her to touch him?

Foreplay didn't seem to be his gig. Not that it'd bothered Jules in the least. The man was *hot*. He'd been fantastic at making *her* feel hot too.

Sleeping against him certainly wasn't a chore, either. He hadn't really held her, but Jules had woken with his arm strewn across her body as if he owned her. Totally Hugh, but somehow, she didn't mind. That should piss her off. It didn't.

Jules shook her head and called herself every name in the book.

The anger she'd felt when she'd been shouting at him in the courtyard was nowhere to be found. She couldn't muster it at all.

Why?

Jules sighed. She hadn't even had time to process what had happened with Lachlan. She wanted to help find Bree — Bridei, whatever — bring her to justice for snatching her nephew.

Hugh had snatched *her* and taken off.

What was next?

Was Duncan going to hunt down the Irish chick?

She needed to question Hugh as if he was a twenty-first century witness. Jules was a cop, after all, no matter what century she happened to be in. She could help. *Wanted* to help.

Would her barbarian help?

He had men and resources just like her brother-in-law, and Hugh had *seen* the woman. Maybe he'd seen where she'd gone.

Jules studied his face as he slept. He had no love of anything MacLeod, yet he'd returned Lachlan to Dunvegan unharmed.

Hugh's a good man.

It wasn't difficult to swallow that idea.

She reached out, wanting to caress his stubble, but paused before making contact with his strong jaw line.

His eyes flew open. "Juliette."

Jules jumped and yanked her hand back. "Sorry."

Hugh shook his head and sat up. "I dinnae mean ta startle ye. Somethin' wrong?" His voice was thick with sleep, and he looked around the room. Like he was about to pounce on whatever had disturbed her.

"No. I...just woke up."

His big shoulders relaxed into the bed and his chest heaved as if he'd released a breath. "Juliette." Her name on his lips made her shiver.

She didn't fight him when Hugh reached for her, tugging her to him. Jules swallowed a whimper when his bare chest came into contact with her breasts. He felt so *good* against her it scrambled her brains.

"I need ta hold ye."

Jules froze. Her stomach quivered. Of course, he didn't *ask* but it didn't bother her like it should. She wanted him to hold her.

He said need, not want.

Their gazes locked in the dim room.

Her gut told her Hugh didn't hold his lovers. Perhaps they didn't even normally share his bed all night. Yet this was the second time Jules was here with him.

"I'd like that," she whispered.

His smile stilled her heart and she ordered herself not to read into it—or anything else concerning Hugh MacDonald.

She nestled close to his side, fighting tremors—and unwanted emotion—when she rested her cheek on his hard pec. Sliding her arm across his abs made her want to hold her breath, but she didn't feel awkward, she felt…overwhelmed. Wanted her body against his. To touch every inch of bare skin she could.

Hugh groaned, but she didn't look up at him.

She couldn't.

He muttered something in Gaelic she didn't have the guts to ask what it meant, then sighed, as if he was content.

Jules' eyes closed of their own accord when he started rubbing her back. It was too good and made her want him even more with every caress of his callused hands. Long, soothing strokes that aroused, yet lulled. She melted into him.

"Lass, yer soft. Ye feel…perfect."

The pause made her pulse skip.

She lifted her head and propped herself up on one elbow to look at him. "You're not so bad, yourself."

Hugh chuckled and it roused her from her stupid sentiments as she felt it rumble beneath her.

"I thought I was. I believe ye said ye'd rather have…wha' did ye call it? Night terrors than be wit' me?"

Jules laughed. She couldn't help it. Composure washed over her, and she gripped it with both hands. She felt better, not so scattered.

She couldn't get swept away in this man, no matter what he'd made her feel physically.

No. Not 'can't'. I won't. It's just sex. I can deal with that.

"Yeah, well, turns out I lied."

Hugh grinned and cupped her cheek with one huge hand. "I dinnae complain abou' tha' untruth." The warmth of his palm sank into her, just like it had when he'd rubbed her back.

Jules tried to ignore it and smiled back at him. "I did enjoy being with you. Am enjoying it, even."

He said nothing, but his thumb moved back and forth over her cheekbone, and she trembled.

Why was it he could barely touch her, and her insides were like a pinball machine for him?

She lit up like he'd hit the grand prize. Jules throbbed for him. Her breasts were heavy on his chest and her nipples tingled.

Jules fought the cloud of lust. "Thank you for

bringing my nephew home. I didn't get a chance to mention it before."

Hugh smirked, probably because she'd not said the *why*.

Kidnapping will delay ya every time. Oh, so will hot sex.

She rolled her eyes at her inner monologue and focused on what her lover was saying.

"Bairns are ta be protected."

She nodded. "Well, thanks anyway. I mean it. My sister wouldn't have survived losing him."

He averted his gaze.

Heaviness settled over them and it only took a half a second for it to occur to Jules what'd come out of her mouth.

Hugh had had to survive the loss of *his* child, and his wife.

Jesus. Foot-in-mouth anyone?

"Uh, sorry." She made her mouth form the words.

Hugh finally looked at her again, but his hand had fallen away from her face. "I dinnae regret bringin' the bairn home. Nay mother should have ta lose her child."

She didn't know what to say. Definitely wouldn't mention it was the same for a father. Last time he'd talked about his past, he'd run from her. Jules didn't want that—especially now. When she was in his arms. "Maybe you and Duncan could be friends now."

Hugh scowled.

Jules bit her bottom lip to keep a laugh in. She'd

only been half-serious. At least the subject change had worked. "We have to find Bree."

"Ye ken a' the Irish lass?"

"Yes. She's the reason I'm here."

He arched an eyebrow and tucked a hand behind his head, elbow bent. With the other one, he tugged Jules closer and settled his large palm at her waist. "Aye?"

She tried not to get swept back into his heat, his touch.

Nodding, Jules launched into Claire's arrival in Scotland, disappearance, then stumbling naked into her arms on the beach when she'd come to look for her.

Hugh was silent as she explained the newspaper article and Bree finding her. Then learning the truth about her Irish *friend* when she'd been at Dunvegan.

She told him about Alana and Xander being Fae, silently apologizing to her sister and the MacLeods—just in case it was a secret. It was Jules' turn to quirk an eyebrow when he didn't look all that surprised.

"I dinnae ken abou' the warrior, but 'tis been rumored tha laird's wife is Fae since her arrival almost three years ago. People thought his lad was a bastard, yet she claimed him. Questions always arise when 'tis abou' heirs."

"Well, keep it to yourself, okay? I don't know if I was allowed to tell anyone."

He shrugged but Jules didn't think he'd run off to blab to his clan there were Fae alive and well on Skye.

Most of them probably didn't believe in magic anyway — she could hope.

"Why would tha lass take Duncan MacLeod's bairn?"

"They think she blames Duncan for the death of her pirate lover, evidently."

"Did he kill him?"

"No. The Fae did." Jules told him about Claire and Duncan's adventure to the Realm of the Fae to rescue Alex and Alana.

He seemed to take everything in stride — including the funky-colored-tree part of the story.

"We have to find her, Hugh. She's dangerous."

"Tha bairn has been returned."

"Right, but what if she tries again? Or does something else? Alana and Xander didn't sense her magic until after she was gone with Lachlan. She came *inside* my sister's home to take her child. Despite all the soldiers and a huge, guarded gate."

"Ye have a point."

Fear rippled over her as Jules' imagination ran wild with everything Bree could do if she popped up again. Jules bit her bottom lip.

"Lass." Hugh's voice yanked her from her inner turmoil. "Dinnae fash. The MacLeods shall find her."

"But I want to help, Hugh." At least he had the decency to hide whatever skepticism he might feel. "I'm a cop. A detective actually. I investigate crimes for a living." Jules gestured to herself and explained what her job was.

The respect shining in his dark eyes made her heart pound.

Her barbarian respected, not scorned, her very un-seventeenth-century-like role at home?

She resisted the urge to kiss him.

"What can I do?" His whisper was thick and made Jules even more of an emotional wreck over him.

He was *sincere*.

"Tell me what you remember about what happened. *Everything* you can remember."

When he was done relaying what he'd seen, disappointment roiled her gut. Bree had used magic to get away from him, and Hugh could only remember where she'd come from with Lachlan, but there'd been no tracks when he'd searched after she'd *poofed*—either direction.

Perhaps Jules had been foolish to assume her modern-day knowledge could help against something she'd considered unreal most of her life. "Dammit," she mumbled.

Hugh cupped her cheeks and forced her to look at him. "Lass, dinnae fash."

"How can I not?"

He slipped his hand to the back of her neck and tugged.

Their lips met and Jules overheated immediately, even before she opened for him.

Hugh's hands slid over her shoulders and down

her back. He gripped her waist, tugging her on top of his body.

She told herself not to get lost in him, but failed when his tongue coaxed hers and his fingers kneaded her ass.

He lifted his head, pushing harder, kissing her deeper, and she was helpless to do anything but let him.

Jules moaned and straddled him, leaning down to get closer as their kiss went on. She wrapped her arms around his neck and flattened her breasts to his chest.

She needed him. Needed *more.*

"Ye dinnae be fashin' now, are ye lass?" Hugh panted as he pulled away, his dark gaze almost black with desire as he searched her face.

His erection seared her pelvis, and her sex bloomed, pulsing because he wasn't in the right place.

Jules shook her head. "More," she demanded, pressing the word into his mouth as she kissed him again.

Hugh flipped them and growled, shoving inside her with a hard thrust.

She held on tight as he proceeded to give her what she wanted.

chapter sixteen

olin!" Hugh strode across the bailey, barely throwing a nod to those of his men-at-arms who greeted him. It was early. The sun barely crested the horizon. He'd left his bed and dressed before his foundling had woken.

His Juliette.

She'd been fantastic. The night had been too short. He'd taken her four times, but a dozen wouldn't have been enough.

His cousin hopped off the wall and dashed to him. "My laird?"

"Gather a dozen men and mount up. Make sure Dubh is ready as well."

His cousin shouted orders to their kinsmen and grabbed a lad to send to the stables for their horses without question. "Where're we goin'?"

"We seek a bairn thief."

Colin's blue eyes widened. "A bairn thief?"

"Aye, I'll explain when we're gathered."

He didn't have to wait long for his kinsmen to assemble, and Hugh thanked the lad that'd brought Dubh to him. He mounted and looked at the faces of the men Colin has selected. They were all his cousins, some more distant than others. All MacDonalds by blood.

Squaring his shoulders, he met each of them in the eye. Some were born at Armadale like him, and some had come and sworn him fealty. "Lads, we need ta find an Irish lass who stole a MacLeod bairn yesterday."

As Hugh launched into the story of the day before, he skirted as many of the parts involving magic as he could.

Mab had raised him to believe in legend, but not all his clansmen believed Fae and magic were real. He'd not want any of them to be afraid to join him in the search.

He'd tell Colin all the details, but the others had no need to know.

"The lass is hiding. The MacLeods dinnae find her on their own lands. I've reason ta believe she's stowed away on our lands."

That roused a few angry yells.

"Do ye think a MacDonald holding is harboring her, my laird?" one asked.

"Nay. I dinnae think they're aware if she's on one a' our farms."

"Let us find her, then!" Colin's declaration had his men rallying, shoving fists into the air and hollering battle cries in Gaelic.

Hugh smiled. "Thank ye, lads! Let us ride!"

Another round of assent rippled through his men.

He gestured for his cousin to lead and turned

Dubh to the gates. Hugh glanced over his shoulder and looked up at his home. Even from the bailey he knew which window was his, and his eyes rested there.

Heavy drapes were still drawn tight, although now the sun was up, greeting a clear, cool morning. The wind shifted his hair against his shoulders, and he couldn't tear his gaze away from the windows. His lass slept in his bed, and he had every intention of keeping her there.

Hugh hadn't liked the desperation in those green eyes the night before when she'd been talking about the seer witch.

So, he'd find the Irish bairn thief. Take her to Dunvegan.

He could do that for Juliette.

Hugh *would* do it, so she'd smile as he held her in the circle of his arms.

"Come, laddie, now we've to catch up!"

Dubh whinnied as he obliged, shooting out the gates and down the wide road.

Juliette's face danced into his mind as he rode hard to catch his men.

Before the sun set, he'd have the Irish lass, and his foundling would have no worries.

Waking up alone had never been her favorite way to greet the morning after sex, especially the best sex of her life.

"Best sex of your life?" Her voice was a sarcastic croak, and Jules scowled.

Only truth rebounded in her brain, which made her feel worse.

Hugh was *fantastic.*

She scoffed and shook her head. Her hair tickled her bare neck and back. Jules gathered up her natural waves, trying to make some sort of order of the mess. Running her fingers through tangles only resulted in pain biting back when she pulled.

"He's gone."

What the hell does that mean?

"It doesn't mean anything." Jules screamed at herself to chill the hell out.

She took a breath and looked around the big room. Her clothes rested where they'd been tossed the day before. Corset on the floor near the window, pants—trews, they were called here—and the shirt not far from each other. One of her boots was visible, the other wasn't.

That'd be fun to find, huh?

Jules sighed and pushed to her feet. Her body ached, especially between her legs, but she regretted *nothing.* That should give her pause, but she didn't give a damn.

She stretched her arms and spine. Sore muscles stood up and said *hello.* It was a good ache, like she'd worked out.

Her bladder roared to be relieved, and so far she wasn't a fan of the seventeen century requirements for such things, but a girl had to do what a girl had to do.

Hugh was a pretty private person, and since he was the laird, he had his own bathroom off one side of his room. A garderobe, Claire had told her it was called.

In some cases, it was a larger room also doubling as a closet, but Hugh's was small, containing only what passed as a toilet.

She made a face as she finished. Jules wanted to bathe. A night of sex made it undesirable to put her clothes on without clean skin. Not to mention tangled hair. She needed to wash it.

The door to Hugh's room flew open without a knock and Jules screamed.

"Lass, 'tis jus' me." Mab's voice didn't make her feel any better.

She was in her birthday suit in the middle of the room. Jules made a dash to the bed and wrapped herself in MacDonald plaid, but Hugh's aunt had seen it all. Heat crept up her neck when she met the dark eyes that were so like her lover's.

If Mab had any doubt Jules had had sex with him, it was now gone.

Hugh's aunt had one bushy eyebrow arched. "Ye've got nothin' I dinnae have, though mine dinnae look as good as yers anamore."

Jules bit the inside of her cheek to keep from laughing. She wasn't about to comment. Besides, Mab had just given her a compliment.

"I'm glad ta see ya, lass. My lad has been mopin' abou' since ye went. Are ye well?"

Moping about?

Hugh?

No way.

She cleared her throat. "I'm good. Thanks. I'd like a bath, though."

"A'course. I'll have tha lads light a fire and bring water fer the tub. Then we'll get ye fed an' dressed." Mab went to hobble out.

"Mab?"

"Aye, lass?"

"Uh…where's Hugh?"

"Gone."

"Gone?"

"Aye, mounted up a' dawn an' left Armadale."

"Where did he go?" Jules tried not to slump as she leaned into the side of the bed. He'd left her…*again?*

Mixed emotions churned in her gut.

The older woman frowned. "He dinnae say, lass."

"So, you don't know when he'll be back, either?"

"Nay, lass. I am sorry. But I dare say he dinnae stray far from yer side now tha' he has ye back. I expect him a 'fore nightfall." The old woman smiled. "I'll get yer bath ordered."

She was gone before Jules could assure her Hugh *didn't* have her back — whatever the hell that meant.

"I still need to go home." She was talking to

herself.

Dammit.

Why had he left without a word?

Jules growled.

As it turned out, her day consisted of nail biting—which was not a normal habit of hers—and a shit load of pacing. She'd stayed in his room, had her bath, which she was too knotted up to enjoy, then gone down to get some food.

Pacing continued in the great hall by the large hearth, then out in the bailey. Jules was too bothered by Hugh's disappearance; she didn't even take the day to explore Armadale like she'd done at Dunvegan her second morning there.

Of course, Claire had shown her around. Her sister's years' long love of historical Scotland had shone in her green eyes as she talked about the castle that had become her home.

Jules kept having to swallow yawns, too. The night had consisted of Hugh inside her more than it had sleep. She could have gone up and crawled in that big bed for a nap, but her mind was spinning a hundred miles an hour.

She was full of chaos—everything Bree—everything Hugh—and the helplessness of being left home like the kid too young to ride the coasters at the amusement park.

"Ugh!" She made a fist with her shout, which only resulted in odd looks from the girls tidying the great hall, so Jules slipped outside. She should've offered to help them like she'd helped Claire, but she couldn't find the words.

Damn man had her twisted up.

Which just pissed her off.

Jules wandered around inside the gates, finally settling on watching the blacksmith work. He was a quiet man named Niall and said he didn't mind. He was making some household things, a new kettle for Mab among other kitchen utensils, and even answered a few questions she'd asked.

He had a kind smile to go with his blue eyes and graying hair, and he was a big guy like the rest of the Highlanders, although his years had filled out his middle.

When Niall spoke of Hugh, Jules heard the adoration in his thick brogue. The man had told her what a good leader Hugh was. As a matter of fact, all the MacDonalds she'd interacted with loved their laird. It was more than clan fealty. They *loved* her barbarian.

Hugh's a good man.

The idea was even easier to swallow than the night before.

A shout went up and she jumped.

"The men are comin' back, now, lass. The laird should be leadin'." Niall flashed a knowing smile that should have irritated her.

Jules hated being transparent. She mustered a nod for him, returned his smile, and dashed for the gate.

chapter seventeen

his sense of defeat melted away when he saw the honey-haired lass rushing to his side. They hadn't found the bairn thief, nor any sign of anyone making camp on MacDonald lands. They'd questioned all his clansmen who held outer farms, and even stopped on MacInnes lands to speak to herders that were out with their flocks.

Nothing.

Of course, it wasn't a shocker that the lass was probably hiding, concealing herself with magic. They'd even scoured the many caves on the section of Skye beach that belonged to his clan.

Hugh had stopped short of MacLeod lands, but he was kicking himself now, since it'd been a force of habit.

Duncan and Alex MacLeod wouldn't have begrudged him for being in their territory if he'd found the seer wench they also sought.

Juliette stopped a few feet from Hugh and Dubh. When he dismounted, he couldn't keep his eyes off her face. Anger dominated her visage, and his foundling perched her hands on her hips. Her shoulders were as tight as the glare she was wearing.

Memories of her naked in his arms darted into his thoughts and Hugh swallowed when his cock twitched. If the look on her face was any indication, Juliette wouldn't be falling bare at his feet any time soon.

"Where the hell do you get off? You. Left. Me."

His clansmen shifted on their feet, and there were several cleared throats. Hugh was keenly aware the wretches didn't scatter or head to the stables with their horses.

No, they *wanted* to watch.

Damn them.

Hugh didn't look at his kin. He didn't tear his eyes from his foundling. He'd gone out *for* her.

Why was she so cross with him?

"Leavin' ye?"

"Yes. *All* day. Without a word, like I'm an errant child."

He laughed; couldn't help it. "Yer wrong, lass."

"I'm wrong? *How?* Have I not been here alone all day?"

Hugh tilted his head to one side. "Alone? Mab dinnae take care a' ye properly? Do I need ta have words wit' my aunt?"

Juliette narrowed her eyes. "Are you making fun of me?"

"I dinnae what ye mean, lass."

"A jest," she snapped. "Are you making a jest out of me?"

Hugh shook his head and closed the distance between them, but he didn't touch her. Not yet.

"Hugh, why did you leave me?" Juliette's tone was a mixture of anger and something else.

Is she hurt?

"I dinnae leave *ye*, lass. I left ta search fer the bairn thief."

"What?"

"I wanted ta find her fer ye, lass."

Juliette's irritated expression faded, and she threw herself into his arms.

Hugh caught her up and kissed her. He couldn't help himself, despite being surrounded by his clansmen.

A few of them chuckled, but none left.

Still.

At the moment he couldn't bring himself to mind.

Juliette wrapped her arms around his neck and kissed him back.

He was hard and aching by the time their mouths parted, and she slid down the front of his body. He wanted to toss her over his shoulder and sprint for his rooms, throw her on his bed and take her like he had the night before. His heart skipped when he saw her misty green eyes.

"You…you…did that for me?"

"Anathin' fer ye, lass." He meant every word. Truth washed over him, and should have alarmed him, but it didn't.

She swallowed and he wanted to kiss her throat.

"Thank you, Hugh." Juliette put her palms on his chest.

"It yielded nothin'." Regret coated his words. Hugh gripped her hands and kissed her knuckles. "I wish we'd have found the lass."

"It's okay. If we work together, we'll find her."

"I am sorry I failed ye."

"You didn't fail me. I just wish you would've said something. I want to help. I told you that last night." The last part of her statement was a censure.

"I wanted ta surprise ye, lass. Ease yer mind. But I hear yer plea."

Hope flared in those emerald eyes and his heart galloped. "Can we try again tomorrow?"

"Aye, lass."

"And I can come, too?" Her question came with narrowed eyes.

A dare.

Hugh couldn't refuse her. "Aye, Juliette. Ye may accompany tha search party."

As Jules looked up into his face, her resolve to stay angry at him for the rest of the night melted away.

Hugh hadn't run from her.

He'd been doing something *for* her, but he really should've included her.

Hadn't they made headway last night?

Never in a million years would Jules have fathomed he be out searching for Bree.

Hugh was supposed to respect her now. She'd explained in detail what she'd made her career. He'd asked questions. Said he'd understood. The respect she'd seen in those dark eyes wasn't her imagination, was it?

Ugh.

Men.

No…barbarians.

Just her luck she'd snagged one.

Right now, she wanted to throw him in the moat.

Why the hell had she rushed into his arms like a damsel in distress the moment he'd told her *why* he'd been gone all day?

Jules had kissed him back for good measure, too.

She rolled her eyes at herself.

He held her loosely even now, his heat sinking into her body, making her remember last night and how it'd felt to be skin to skin with her barbarian. Her sex throbbed as desire spread down her limbs, settling low in her belly, and wobbling her legs.

Hugh was interested, too, his erection against her pelvis.

How could she want to kiss him and kill him at the same time?

"You promise?" Jules made herself demand, glaring into that handsome face.

There was appealing stubble highlighting his strong planes, but she told the urge to run her fingers over his skin to go to hell.

"Aye, lass. Ye've my word."

She nodded but didn't pull away when he cupped her face and his dark eyes compelled her, pinning her where she stood.

Jules' heart kicked up a notch as she waited for him to dip down and take her mouth.

He didn't. "I dinnae give my word, lightly, lass."

Her breath caught and she swallowed. "I...I...know. Thank you. I appreciate you listening to me."

"Always, lass." The truth of his words rolled over her form, and she shivered.

She couldn't relax, even as Hugh smiled. Butterflies started a cyclone in her stomach, and she screamed at herself to get it together.

Spending the day without him had, in a way, shown her what a good man her barbarian could be. Showing was always better than telling, and his people adored him.

What could be a better example than that?

She'd always been a sucker for a good, strong leader.

Of course, her barbarian tipped the *pushy bastard* scales too much for her liking, but she hadn't minded the *take-charge* in bed, despite her internal control freak.

Hugh's eyes hadn't moved from her face, and they

stood glued to each other, chest to breasts, hips to hips.

Jules was aware of all the gazes on them, but as he finally lowered his head and pressed his lips to hers, she couldn't bring herself to give a shit.

She opened for him and kissed him back with all her might, squeezing her arms around his neck and shimmying as close as she could get.

Warning sirens went off in the back of her head.

One night in this man's arms, now she was being a PDA queen—which she'd always hated. She didn't need verbal confirmation that she'd fall into his bed and take him back into her body again tonight. As many times as she could.

It's just sex.

Was it?

As conscious thought lost to the desire clouding her brain, Jules could only settle on one thing.

Hugh MacDonald was dangerous.

She was in serious trouble now.

Oh, shit.

chapter eighteen

Jules slipped one leg into her trews as silently as she could manage, cursing when she lost her balance and her bare foot hit the stone floor with a *slap*. She righted herself and glanced at the bed, but Hugh hadn't moved.

She chided herself for her lingering gaze.

He was naked and delicious, and they'd had sex twice. The MacDonald tartan was slung low on his body, woven between his legs, baring one thigh and half of his perfect ass.

A tremor shot down her spine as her body tingled from the memories.

I need to go.

If she had any chance, it was now, before the sun was up. Jules remembered the way to Dunvegan. She couldn't make it there on foot, but if she had a horse—

"No. He'd kill me."

Of course, there were horses other than Dubh in the stables, but if she took Hugh's stallion, it'd be a personal insult. Something she needed.

Maybe he'd be so angry it could banish the way he'd looked at her the past few days. Make him push her away; make her forget the tenderness in his dark eyes. Make Jules forget what it was like to touch him, kiss him. Have him hold her.

She crushed her eyes shut and cursed the tears that threatened.

Damn Hugh MacDonald for making her question her mission.

She had to get home, even without Claire.

Why on *earth* had she told Claire and Duncan she wanted to *stay* at Armadale that day?

She'd called off her own rescue party, after all.

Because I wanted to keep them from going to war.

Liar.

Because I want to stay with Hugh.

Jules shoved her feet into her boots, ignoring how her chest ached. She didn't want to walk away from him, but she had to.

Then she'd have to walk away from her sister, the only family she had. She'd written letters to Claire a few times in the week and a half she'd been at Armadale, and her sister had written back every time, never once asking when she was coming back to Dunvegan—or if she was still planning on going home.

Claire only asked if she was okay, and if Hugh was treating her well. She'd even demanded to be told if she needed to come and kick his ass. That'd made Jules snicker—then and now.

She finished dressing and stood at the end of the bed she'd shared with him every night since she'd arrived.

Jules had to go. Now.

She was already in too deep with Hugh MacDonald.

The longer she stayed, the harder it'd be to walk away.

She wanted to kiss him goodbye, or at least touch him again, but she couldn't. Hugh had this uncanny ability to wake up right before she'd made contact with his skin. He'd done it a few times. Then they'd talk, kiss, and make love again.

Jules fought the tremors inching down her spine. Remembering what it was like with him wouldn't do anything except make her lose her clothes and climb back in that big bed. She crept to the door, wincing every time her boots creaked. Her hand shook as she pushed the rough wood open and slipped into the corridor.

One tear slid down her cheek, but she ignored it and kept moving.

Paranoia ate at her all the way down the stairs and across the bailey. Torches perched every few feet along the wall of the embattlement caught her attention and made her curse.

How was she going to get outside the gates?

Jules sucked in a breath and jogged to the stables. She'd worry about it when she had a horse.

No one was around.

Soft snoring greeted her ears, and she glanced up.

The stable boy—or boys—must be asleep in the

loft, and she didn't have much time. Waking someone wasn't going to go over well, and Jules still had the MacDonalds at the gate to contend with.

They would be awake, on night watch.

"Dammit." She inched forward, cringing when her boots crunched over discarded hay on the stable's dirt floor. "Dubh." Her whisper made her cringe, too.

Then a soft neigh greeted her ears.

She called him again. Jules didn't know what stall he was in, and it was dark.

Reallllllllly dark.

Feeling around the place, somehow, she managed not to fall on her ass. Every horse she walked by shifted or neighed.

Finally, she found him—or rather, he found her. Jules called his name a third time, and Dubh bumped her outstretched hand with his muzzle.

"I gotta go, boy. Can you take me?" She rested her forehead against his wider one, and the stallion lipped her palm. She rubbed his baby-soft nose and sighed.

I don't want to go.

Jules opened the stall, holding her breath when the wood protested with a loud creak.

Dubh followed her out of the stable and across the bailey with no more than her hand on his neck.

She glanced up at his tall back. She was going to have to haul her ass up there, but she'd wait until she assessed the gate sitch. If Jules couldn't convince the guard to let her leave—and she hadn't even contemplated the *how* – it was *game over* anyways.

Maybe the horse route was foolish. She could have snuck out on foot much easier.

"Who goes there?" A deep voice demanded.

Jules swallowed and straightened her shoulders. She bit back a cry of relief when she made out Colin MacDonald in the darkness.

He stepped toward her, a lit torch in hand. Fire illuminated the handsome planes of his face. His dark brows were drawn tight, but his blue eyes were kind, like always. "My lady?"

"Colin. I-I-I need to go."

Silence.

Her stomach somersaulted.

"The laird dinnae ken." It was a statement, not a question.

"No, he's sleeping."

"I dinnae *let* ye leave, my lady."

He means shouldn't, and that's better than can't.

"I…can't stay anymore, Colin. I have to go home."

His mouth set in a hard line, and Jules' heart sank. He wasn't going to let her out.

"He'll come after ye, my lady."

"Probably. But I'll be gone by then."

Colin held a torch higher. "Ye've Dubh, my lady."

"Yeah."

Shock rolled over her when Hugh's cousin grinned.

"He'll be angry. Verra angry." His statement was

wrapped in amusement.

"I don't want you to be in trouble with him. This is all on me. Can you tell him I knocked you out, or something?"

Colin chuckled. "'Tis certainly tha safest thing fer me."

Jules relaxed a tad. "So, you're gonna let me go?"

"Aye."

She blew out a breath and swallowed. "Thank you, Colin."

Hugh's cousin nodded and helped hoist her to Dubh's back.

Jules thanked him again.

"Ye are verra good fer my cousin, my lady. I am sad ta see ye go."

Jules wove her hands in Dubh's thick mane and swallowed against the lump in her throat. "I wouldn't if I didn't have to, believe me." Emotion made her words shake and she frowned.

That's not true, is it?

Colin opened the gates and Dubh darted out, cantering down the long road without much urging.

She didn't give in to the desire to look over her shoulder.

Jules *couldn't* look back.

If she did, she'd lose her nerve and turn around.

Hugh awoke alone, but her scent lingered all around him. His pillows, his plaid, and the other blankets on his bed, it was all Juliette. He inhaled and closed his eyes. He could drown in her. Happily.

He stretched and reached. Hugh frowned when the linens he encountered were cold. She'd left his bed some time ago.

Sitting up, he swallowed a yawn and looked around the room. "Juliette?"

The lack of an answer had his frown slipping to a scowl.

Hugh threw his legs over the side of his bed and shoved to his feet so fast his head reeled.

Where is she?

His clothing was strewn all over the floor, but *hers* wasn't in sight.

"Juliette?" He made his voice louder, but his gut said she was gone. Hugh cursed and whipped his trews off the floor.

Shoving his legs in probably took more time than if he would've just taken a breath and dressed at a normal pace—because he'd missed twice and almost tripped.

He tugged a fresh leine overhead and strapped his sword on with jerky hands. His heart was thundering, but he ignored that—and what it could mean.

Hugh stormed out into the corridor and slammed his door shut. He stomped down into the great hall, only to be met with emptiness.

"Juliette!" His call echoed.

The sun was up—but barely so, if the pale light streaming in the big window, was any indication.

Hugh stalked to the kitchens, yelling her name as he went.

There was already activity there—lasses preparing to feed the men when they woke.

He doubted his foundling was there, but perhaps someone had seen her.

"Hugh MacDonald, wha' are ye hollerin' abou' at this hour?" Aunt Mab's voice was as cross as her expression when he whirled around and met her dark gaze. His aunt had one hand propped on one ample hip, and the other planted on her cane. She stood in the doorway leading to the kitchens, blocking his way.

"Have ye seen Juliette?" he barked.

"Nay. Dinnae she be wit' ye?"

"Would I be lookin' fer her if she was?"

Mab frowned. "Dinnae speak ta me like tha'."

Irritation rolled over him, but Hugh sighed. "Have ye seen her?"

"Nay."

He cursed long and loud, and his aunt ranted about his language. Instead of answering the woman who'd raised him, he spun away and stalked out toward the bailey.

No clansman he encountered had seen his lover.

Juliette was nowhere to be found—inside or outside of Armadale.

That meant she'd fled.

Damn good thing he knew her destination.

But why now?

Things had been good the night before, despite their daily searches failing to locate the Irish bairn thief over the past week and a half. Word from the MacLeods confirmed they hadn't found her, either. Both clans continued to search.

Last night was more *than good.*

They'd talked, laughed, and he'd taken her twice. She'd not complained about anything. Juliette had even kissed him long and hard before they'd gone to sleep. He'd held her in his arms like every night since he'd brought her back.

Was she upset his men had failed to locate the Irish lass?

Hugh rammed his hand through his hair and shook his head. He'd just have to ask her.

When he got her back.

His conscience chided that he should let Juliette choose.

He couldn't snatch her a third time. He should've let her choose from the beginning. He'd brought her to Armadale — twice — against her will.

Should he let her go?

Juliette had said multiple times she needed to get home. She didn't mean Dunvegan.

The future.

Full of things he couldn't even fathom, although

he'd listened with rapt attention any time Juliette had told him of the world she lived in.

Hugh didn't want to let her go.

He jogged to the stables and hollered for the lad to ready Dubh. He was greeted with a hasty, "Aye, my laird." Then paced while he waited.

"My laird." The lad skittered to a halt in front of him, with no black stallion on his heels.

Hugh steadied him with a hand to his thin shoulder. "Lad? What's wrong?"

"Dubh dinnae be here, my laird."

"Wha—" Hugh blinked. It didn't take long to figure out—Juliette had taken *his* horse?

He should be angry as hell, but he threw his head back and laughed.

Big brown eyes were as wide as they could go when he met the lad's gaze. "My laird?"

"Weeel, go on, laddie, get me another horse."

"Oh!" The lad jumped. "Aye, my laird."

Hugh rode to the gates on a dark brown mare Dubh had sired. She wasn't as good as his stallion, but she was fast. He took one look at the guilt on his cousin Colin's face and narrowed his eyes. "Ye, I will deal wit' later."

Colin had the decency to nod, but Hugh didn't like the twinkle in his eyes.

He nudged the mare forward and she darted down the road.

chapter nineteen

She heard his deerskin boots on the loamy ground even before she caught his now-familiar scent. In her peripheral vision she saw him tell the other horse to go home.

He gave it a smack on the ass, and it darted the way he'd come.

Jules closed her eyes and hugged her knees closer to her breasts in the borrowed leine and trews. She'd left Claire's black corset in Hugh's room, so at least she could breathe.

Dubh snorted and hooved the rocky sand, as if he felt her nerves. Or maybe he was greeting his master. He tossed his head like he was beckoning Hugh.

She wanted to glare at him. "Traitor," she said under her breath.

The stallion moved toward the laird, nuzzling Hugh's leine-covered chest.

Her barbarian patted Dubh's wide forehead, running his hands under the horse's wide jowls, and whispering to him.

Jules studied the surface of the water, watching the waves crash into each other before they hit the shore, over and over. "Are you angry with me?" She felt

Hugh's body heat at her back.

"Nay." He grunted as he lowered his large frame to the sand beside her.

"Really?" She risked a side-glance at his handsome face.

The tenderness in those dark eyes made her heart skip.

Don't look at me like that.

"Dubh will always return ta me," Hugh said, the barest hint of a smile on his tempting mouth.

Jules wanted to ask, *"What about me?"*

She couldn't speak. A lump dominated her throat.

Wind tossed the loose waves of her hair in her face, and he beat her to tucking the strands behind her ear. The touch made her want more.

"I reckoned ye would go ta Dunvegan," he said.

She sighed. "That was the plan."

"Then?"

Jules shook her head, averted her eyes, and tried to stave off tears.

"Lass? Wha' happened?" His low voice was a demand that should've irritated her, but it only made her stomach flutter.

"You happened." Jules cursed the confession.

Hugh said nothing, but she didn't fight him when he slid his arm around her shoulders and tugged her close. His warmth bled into her side, through the rough material of seventeenth century garments.

She wanted to throw her arms around him, bury

her face against his massive chest. Melt into him. Beg him to kiss her, touch her again. "I can't stay here." Desperation wrapped the words even to her own ears.

He'd know she didn't mean the beach.

"So ye've said." Hugh was matter-of-fact. No hint to what he was thinking.

Or feeling.

Jules bit back a whimper.

He cupped her cheeks and tilted up. So, she had no choice but to meet those dark eyes. Deep pools of midnight. Hugh's gaze raked her face. Her barbarian said nothing, but those lush lips parted, and her heart kicked up.

When he dipped his head down, Jules met his kiss, instead of pulling away like she should. She fell into him like always. Opened for him without hesitation, shifting into the circle of his arms as his tongue enticed hers.

Emotion threatened to swallow her whole. Jules pushed it all away, gathering physical feeling to her, and kissed him harder.

Hugh rose to his knees in the sand, and she went with him, slipping her arms around his neck as their tongues danced and dueled.

She groaned and nestled closer.

He ended the kiss and stared.

They didn't speak, but Jules didn't need to hear his voice. He wanted her; she could read it in his face — as well as feel his erection against her stomach.

However, his expression, other unnamed emotions in his eyes made her heart somersault.

Hugh was always so implacable.

What's changed?

Am I really seeing…feeling… in his eyes?

No. Do not read into that.

Hugh's large, callused hands tugged her leine at the waist of her breeches.

Jules lifted her arms obediently, and he slowly took the baggy shirt from her body. She didn't care that it was bright out, full morning now that the sun was up. Or that they were on the beach, in the open, where anyone could see them.

She just wanted him.

The chilly sea air kissed her skin, stinging her nipples as they hardened. Then he was there, cupping and kneading her bare breasts, shooting desire to her core. She throbbed for him already.

He caressed her neck and kissed her collarbone, nibbling on the hollow of her throat before taking her mouth again. Soft and sweet, and totally unlike any other time he'd kissed her. Languorous heat engulfed Jules' whole form and her thighs shook, threatening to collapse.

As if he sensed it, Hugh pulled her flush to his chest, those big hands all over her bare back. Touching, caressing, soothing. Turning her on in a way she'd never been before. With none of his usual rawness, the roughness that was just her barbarian. It fired her in a different way.

This was…more.

Jules combusted for him from the inside out.

Tears stung her eyes and she tried to look away, but he pulled back and cupped her face.

Hugh thumbed away the first tear. "Lass, why're ye cryin'?"

"I don't know," Jules whispered.

Liar.

She couldn't *not* cry.

Because she'd fallen in love with Hugh MacDonald.

One corner of his kiss-swollen lips shot up. "We dinnae have tears." Then he took her mouth until she was moaning in his arms.

"I want you."

"Tha's my Juliette. Always direct wit' what she wants." The fondness in his voice, in his hazy dark gaze, made her heart thunder in her ears.

Not always.

She didn't have the guts to bare her heart to the man who'd stolen it. Could never admit she wanted nothing more than to be *his* Juliette.

Jules forced a smile, going for sexy and hoped like hell he bought it. "Aye, my barbarian. Now, do I get what I want?"

Hugh chuckled and kissed her again, nipping her bottom lip and then licking away the sting.

She moaned and went in for more, needing to taste

him again. Jules wove her hands in his long dark hair and buried her tongue in his mouth.

When he finally ended their lip-lock, they both panted and her core pulsed. Jules *needed* him.

"Lass, yer tryin' ta slay me," Hugh breathed, his warm breath tickling her cheek.

"I need you. I want you." She tugged at his belt buckle, but her fingers shook so much she couldn't get the job done.

He laughed and gripped her hands, lavishing kisses on her knuckles. "Ye've still too many clothes on. Discard yer trews an' I'll take care a' this."

Jules nodded, sucking in air so she could think, so she wouldn't tumble to the sand in a heap. She pushed to shaking legs and reached for the ties on her pants. She had to try three times before the knot loosened, and she wasted no time pushing them off her hips.

"Hmmm, did I mention tha' I like when ye dress like a lad?" His eyes zoned in below her waist.

She regained her composure and flashed a smile. "Why? No underwear? You guys really have to do something about that." She'd long discarded the semi-panties Claire had made.

"Nay. This is better." Hugh chuckled again and stalked to her, pulling her naked body hard against his—and the jerk was still dressed.

Jules yelped but he kissed her so fast all she could do was kiss him back. She leaned away before she could lose herself in him again. "Hey, no fair. You still have clothes on."

Hugh nuzzled her neck, laying a line of hot wet kisses down to her shoulder and ignored her. His hands ran down her back, squeezing her ass and wrenching another moan from her as his erection teased her pelvis through leather.

"Please…Hugh…babe…"

He paused, arching a dark eyebrow. "Babe?"

Jules panted as he rocked into her. "The word is…a common endearment….in my time."

"Fer a grown man?" Each word was punctuated with a jolt forward, into her. Hugh rubbed her in the right spot, but not with the right pressure.

His fingertips skirted her thigh. The caress was too light, a brush, and he continued on, dragging his hand to part the curls between her legs.

Jules gasped, but her lover ignored it, continuing his too-light ministrations, thumbing the tight bundle of nerves at the top of her sex.

He applied pressure, then took it away.

She wobbled, but he held her tight to him. Her thoughts scattered; her sex ached, empty. Each teasing pass made her feel more unfulfilled, even though her clit throbbed and shot pleasure all over.

Jules needed Hugh inside her. Couldn't gather the words to demand it, let alone answer him.

He kissed her again, until she was a begging blob of need.

Finally, *finally* Hugh left her to grab the

MacDonald plaid from Dubh's back. He laid it in the sand and gestured for her to come to him.

Jules didn't hesitate. She couldn't refuse the heated promise in those eyes, even if he hadn't kissed and touched her to the point of dissolving. She tumbled to the tartan without taking her eyes off the gorgeous man undressing before her. Her greedy eyes ate up every inch of bare skin that came into view.

Broad shoulders, huge defined pecs. His biceps were so thick it took both of her hands to span one. The tight black curls on his chest were just the right amount—not too much, and not too little. Did nothing to detract from his defined lines. He had an eight pack that was nothing like the fake guys she'd seen at the gym and had everything to do with seventeenth century hard work.

Jules loved to drag her fingers through the dark strip of hair dividing that perfection just to watch his abs jump. Then what lay below…she'd never been with a man who could make her body feel like Hugh MacDonald could.

His thighs were hard and thick, sprinkled with dark springy hair she loved to tease. Hugh's ass was made for grabbing.

Tremors racked Jules' frame as she watched him. She bit her bottom lip to keep from crying out—all she could see—remember—was her legs wrapped in his as they moved together.

"Lass, when ye look a' me like tha'—" His Adam's

apple bobbed.

She quivered. Jules squeezed her thighs together when her core throbbed. *She* had the power to make this tough barbarian fall apart. Lose control. Scream her name.

Her mouth went dry when she focused on his proudly jutting erection. It wouldn't be long, and he would be inside her, they would find completion in each other's arms.

For a little while longer, he's mine.

Pushing away dark thoughts, Jules opened her arms, inviting the man she loved. She didn't want to be apart from him for even a moment longer.

When he settled over her body, it wasn't with his usual roughness. Nor did Hugh part her thighs with impatience—although neither tendency had ever bothered Jules.

She'd never been a fan of too much foreplay. From the start she'd taken him how she could get him, but her heart very much liked this new tender lover side. Jules wanted to burrow into him.

His gaze was intense as he propped himself above her, and she squirmed.

"What's with the sudden patience?" Jules went for a tease, but her voice shook, and her stomach fluttered.

The smile he flashed stole her breath.

He was *beautiful.*

"Enjoyin' the view, s'all."

She'd never been a blusher, but heat seared the

back of her neck, creeping up to her ears. "Make love to me, Hugh."

He didn't answer, but he was quiet—too quiet.

Emotions *were* in his eyes, but Jules couldn't risk believing what she *thought* she saw, even if it was the second time.

Hugh dragged two fingers across her mouth, down her cheek, then her neck. He traced her collarbone and circled a breast, stopping to tease her nipple before doing the same to the other.

Jules' stomach muscles jumped under his feather-light touches as he continued on, and her heart slipped into overdrive.

Like his kisses, Hugh had never touched her like this. Lazy exploration that set her blood well on its way to a rolling boil. Driving her crazy, but she would beg him not to stop if he even dared. She cried out, arching her back when he teased her already swollen clit.

"So wet."

"You're a tease, what'd you expect?"

His chuckle made her moan.

"You're enjoying this way too much." The words were strained. Jules had to force out one after the other.

"Ye dinnae be, my sweet Juliette?"

Affection in that deep voice made her pause, and any response she might've mustered got caught up in her throat.

Silence fell and they stared at each other.

Jules bit back a whimper—or maybe it was a sob.

Hugh caressed her cheek, the smile curving his mouth soft, tender. One she'd never seen before.

"I just want to be with you," she whispered.

He nodded and those dark eyes scorched her from the inside out.

Without another word, Hugh trailed hot kisses down her belly, parting her thighs with his big hands so he could settle between them.

Jules gasped. He'd never —

She called his name with the first swipe of his tongue. A whine was next as he teased her with his fingers, too. She buried her hands in his thick hair, trying not to tug too much, but he was sucking her into his mouth now, taking her higher and higher.

Hugh thrust two fingers inside her as he thumbed her clit and nibbled at the same time.

Jules screamed and threw her head back. Her hips lifted from the plaid of their own accord, but her lover held her still — and down.

He was relentless, licking, sucking, even biting, until none of the words falling from her mouth made any sense.

She moved her head back and forth because Hugh was still holding her tightly as he pleasured her.

"Juliette," he hummed against her skin, and Jules lost control.

She teetered on the edge for only a moment. Her whole body jerked beneath his. Orgasm hit so hard it scrambled her vision and her head swam.

Jules hollered his name and had to remind herself to breathe. Her muscles spasmed. Pleasure made her whole form tingle as the intensity slid back and forth.

Hugh pulled back and ran his hands over her breasts, down her stomach, dragging his fingers over her thighs and knees, even her calves. It soothed but revved her up all over again.

The look on his face was hazy self-satisfaction, as if he'd gotten off on making her come. "Ye screamed my name."

"I have before," Jules panted. She reached for his hand and entwined their fingers because she couldn't *not* touch him.

"It dinnae get old." He winked.

Jules laughed and tugged his hand. "Come to me, Hugh. Be with me."

Make love to me.

She couldn't say *that* out loud again.

"Will ye scream my name again?" He hovered over her, pushing her legs wider with a knee.

"Aye."

He gave her no answer—and no recovery time. Hugh dipped his head down to take her mouth. At the same time, and true to his nature, he positioned his erection at her center. He filled her to the hilt with one hard stroke that made them both gasp.

She rubbed her tongue against his when Hugh started to thrust and wrapped her achy legs around his waist. Tomorrow she was going to hurt in places she didn't know *could* hurt, but right now, Jules didn't give a damn.

Hugh slammed into her over and over, until she struggled to keep up with him, and they both had no rhythm. He held onto her, and Jules clung to him as they moved together.

They needed no words, but emotion was as heady in the air as the pleasure shooting all over her body. Any place with a nerve ending was on fire, and she moaned with every brush of his hands and mouth.

Hugh always made sure she was as into the sex as he was, but this, too, was different. His caresses had meaning, as did every look he gave her.

She bit back *I love you* when their gazes locked.

Jules tilted her face and met his kiss instead, crushing her eyes shut. She lifted into his next surge forward, and the one after that.

Heat bloomed in her lower belly and her core quivered. She moaned as her inner muscles started to contract and relax. Climax hit, but this time it was balanced. There was no urgency, only the pleasure washing over her.

Hugh slowed his thrusts, drawing out her ecstasy and grunting into their fused mouths.

Jules waited for him to exit her body like normal.

He didn't. He stiffened, stilling above her.

His release shot deep inside her, spreading the warmth already dominating her.

He didn't pull out.

Another first that made her heart rebound against her ribs. She swallowed a new wave of emotion as well as the three words playing on the tip of her tongue.

When he collapsed on top of her, Jules held him tight and pressed her mouth to his. He took it from there, kissing her deeply, but tenderly.

She sighed and snuggled into him.

"Lass, let me go, or I'll crush ye." Hugh's words were muffled against her neck, but Jules heard amusement, too.

She managed a sheepish smile and complied — but only a little. Jules didn't want to be parted from him just yet.

Or ever.

Her breath caught when her eyes raked his face.

Hugh's high cheekbones were flushed with color and his mouth red, swollen from hers. Every inch of his gorgeous, muscled frame carried a sheen of sweat, but she didn't care.

I did that to him.

The man she loved was the hottest guy she'd ever seen.

"Wha' is it?" Hugh whispered, brushing her hair from her face.

"Nothing." Jules couldn't tell him she'd miss him. Or face that this was *it* for them. She'd see her sister, kiss the baby, say goodbye, and have the Faery Stones opened so she could go home.

She had to leave now, before she lost her nerve.

Jules dragged her fingers down his damp chest, playing in Hugh's curls until his nipples hardened from the attention.

He smirked, grabbed her hand, and pressed small kisses to her knuckles. "C'mon, lass. I'll take ye ta Dunvegan." When he leaned down to kiss her forehead, Jules sucked back a sob.

"Wh-wh-what?" She fought the urge to throw her arms around his neck, rub her cheek against his rough stubble, cling to him.

Tell him I love him.

Jules averted her eyes. She couldn't tell him how she felt. It wouldn't go over well, and despite their lovemaking just now, her feelings were definitely one-sided.

I'm not ready to go yet.

"'Tis where ye wan' ta be, dinnae?"

His voice jolted her.

Their gazes collided against her will.

She couldn't read his expression, but that was nothing new with Hugh MacDonald.

No. I want to be with you.

"Claire's there," she whispered instead. "I need to say goodbye before I go."

Coward.

The man she loved nodded and pulled Jules gently to her feet without another word.

Pain seared her heart and she looked away from him, searching the loamy ground for her clothes. In her peripheral vision, she saw Hugh doing the same.

Getting dressed was a mechanized thing that left her more chilled than the frigid sea air ever could have. Tremors chased each other down her spine and she fought tears.

Jules still couldn't look at him, so she folded up his plaid, hugging it to her chest before she could muster the courage to hand it over.

She was grateful for the wind whipping her hair around. Made no efforts to brush it from her face. Never had Jules thought he'd actually let her go.

Hugh was willing to take her to Dunvegan.

It was what she wanted. So why the hell did it hurt so badly?

chapter twenty

The ride to his enemy's gates had Hugh's gut so tight it was hard to breathe. He chided himself to relax. The MacLeods meant no harm to his lass. He understood it logically. There was no reason to worry about her once she was inside the safety of Dunvegan.

He grudgingly had to give Duncan and Alex MacLeod their due. They were fierce protectors of what they held dear. Juliette was family to them. They would do their duty to keep her safe in his absence.

Hugh would watch her until he couldn't see her anymore, damn whatever the MacLeod guards had to say about it. After he'd grabbed her from the bailey, they'd never let him inside again. Had the same happened in his courtyard, he'd have acted equally.

If it was allowed, he'd escort her inside, but he had too much pride to beg.

Hugh would never show weakness in front of *any* member of his rival clan.

Juliette's back was stiff against his chest, which didn't help his breathing problem. Her hands clamped onto his wrists, too, but he wasn't about to tell her to release him.

Hell, he'd prefer she *never* released him.

Hugh stilled on Dubh's back. Feelings he'd been avoiding for a week surfaced and his mouth went dry.

He wasn't nervous about leaving Juliette with Clan MacLeod. Hadn't he talked himself into letting her go from the moment he'd left Armadale to look for her?

I don't want to lose her.

I lo —

Hugh shook his head.

Nay.

"Dinnae be it."

"What?" Juliette glanced over her shoulder.

"Nothin'." Hugh cleared his throat and sat straighter.

She tried to turn in his arms to look at him.

His stomach flipped and he forced a frown. "Sit still a 'fore ye knock us both from Dubh's back."

Juliette narrowed her pretty green eyes. "You're a better horseman than that."

He said nothing. She knew him well—too well. "Turn 'round."

"Why? Hugh? What's wrong?" The concern in her voice made his heart speed up.

"Nothin' tha's yer concern."

It was true. How he...*felt* for her mattered not.

Juliette harrumphed, but she did as he'd bid, turning to look ahead. The golden waves of her loose hair tickled his cheek.

Her scent washed over his senses and Hugh closed his eyes, savoring the woman he'd fallen in love with.

While he still could.

He'd have to remember their lovemaking on the beach. Hold it dear, because once Juliette slipped from Dubh's back, he'd never hold her again.

She was going home.

To the far future.

Hugh's throat started to close, and he coughed.

"Are you okay?" Juliette whispered.

"I'm braw."

"I'm not." Her voice was so low he almost missed it.

Emotion jolted Hugh and he had to chide himself to sit still. Unable to gather words, he slipped an arm around her waist and squeezed her against his chest. He kissed her temple and dipped his head down to whisper in her ear. "Everythin' will be well, lass."

She nodded and swallowed.

He studied Juliette's strong profile. Wanted to turn her head and take her mouth but restrained himself.

Silence fell, because God knew Hugh couldn't muster words for his lass.

Coward.

Wretch.

He called out when they approached the outer gate, but two MacLeods still closed the distance with claymores drawn and matching glares on their faces.

Hugh gritted his teeth and bowed from his horse's

back. "I've brought the lass ta see her sister."

The guard on the right, a huge blond man, approached.

At least he has the decency to sheath his sword.

"Good ta see ye again, my lady." He inclined his head to Juliette.

"You too, Cormac."

Jealousy flared up from his gut and Hugh tightened his grip on his lass.

"Hugh, you're hurting me."

"I'm sorry," he muttered, forcing his arm to loosen, but he didn't want to. He wanted to kiss her, show *Cormac* Juliette McGowan was his.

The guard put his hand out to assist her dismount.

The moment she set her palm in the much larger one, an unfamiliar sense of panic washed over Hugh.

He wanted to clutch her to him, whip Dubh around and hie home to Armadale, where Juliette belonged.

In his arms.

In his bed.

For the rest of their lives.

I love her.

Three words became a chant in his head. With each repetition, his chest constricted more. He clenched his jaw until his teeth hurt when Cormac MacLeod helped her down.

A sense of loss, emptiness, stabbed Hugh's chest, and he wanted to flee.

Or kill something.

He was cold without her body heat. Frigid without her against his chest, in his arms. Hugh's wrists burned where she'd gripped him. As if they already missed her touch. His own skin was turning on him.

Juliette stood in front of the MacLeod clansman, looking up at Hugh.

He fought the urge to close his eyes and met her beautiful emerald gaze straight-on. He couldn't kiss her from Dubh's back, and he didn't have the bollocks to dismount and pull her into his arms.

If he did, he wouldn't let her go.

"Lass." He cursed the word as it cracked. Hugh cleared his throat.

Juliette came to him immediately, caressing Dubh's dark neck. She wouldn't meet Hugh's eyes.

He leaned down and brushed her hair from her face. "Juliette."

Finally, she looked up. Those green eyes were misty. Her nose was red, as if she was fighting tears, and her lush lips parted.

His heart plummeted to his stomach. A declaration of love played on his tongue, but he shoved it away. "Be well, Juliette." Hugh's voice shook. It took all he was made of to look down at her like she didn't matter. Like he didn't love her. Didn't ache to keep her.

She bit her swollen bottom lip and nodded. Her breasts heaved as if she'd taken a breath, and she swallowed. "You, too, Hugh. Umm, thanks for…kidnapping me."

Hugh smiled as unwanted sentiment clogged his throat. He dragged two fingers down her cheek. "I've no regrets." However, he did, because he was letting her go.

Juliette flashed a watery smile that stilled his heart. "Neither do I."

Words caught in his throat.

This is what she wants. To go home.

She stepped back, averting her gaze.

Cormac MacLeod slipped his arm around her shoulders to guide her into the bailey, and Hugh wanted to lop it off. Shout at the man to unhand his lass.

She's not mine anymore.

Not that she ever was.

He'd taken her to Armadale against her will— twice.

The other MacLeod guard inclined his dark head when Hugh's eyes rested on him, but he didn't return the gesture.

Without another word, he turned Dubh away from the MacLeod stronghold. His heart thundered as if he'd run down the beach to Dunvegan, and every forced breath was a dagger to his lungs.

He closed his eyes and buried his hand in his stallion's thick mane.

Hugh MacDonald had finally met his match—and now he was riding away from her.

His bitter laugh filled his ears, but he shook his head and kicked his horse. He'd never looked back before, and today was not the day to change his ways.

"Did ye find her?"

Hugh dragged his hand down his face, ignoring the scratch of stubble against his palm. He swallowed a sigh and didn't turn toward the meddling old woman he called aunt. "Aye."

Silence.

Which was never good.

Aunt Mab invaded his ledger room, her cane *tap-tapping* on the floor as she hobbled forward.

Hugh still didn't look at the woman who'd raised him. He couldn't.

"Weeel?"

"Well, wha'?" He tried not to bark. He had no patience for a scolding.

"*Where* is yer lass?"

"Dunvegan, I s'pose."

"Dunvegan? Whye'er fer?" Aunt Mab's voice shot up an octave and Hugh winced.

"Auntie—"

Thwack.

Pain shot into his shoulders, reverberating down his spine. "Jesu!" Hugh shot to his feet and whirled on his tiny aunt, who had her cane poised for another strike. "Ye hit me!"

"Aye, an' shall do so again, if ye dinnae watch yer mouth, lad." She glared up at him, her dark eyes flashing.

"Mab," Hugh growled.

"Sit down a'fore ye hurt yerself," she returned, her expression even darker.

"Myself? I'll hurt ye," Hugh muttered, but he didn't have the bollocks to say it louder. He obeyed, taking the seat he'd been wallowing in at the large table in his ledger room.

His aunt scowled as she took the seat beside the fireplace, despite the warm fire burning brightly. "Go get tha' lass."

"Nay."

"Nay?"

Hugh avoided her narrowed eyes, shifting on the chair. "She's goin' home, Aunt Mab."

"Did ye ask her ta stay?"

A lump clogged his throat, but Hugh shook his head. He still couldn't look at her.

"Why no'?"

He studied his boots until his temples throbbed, so Hugh closed his eyes.

"Speak, lad."

"Nay," he croaked.

"Juliette is not Brenna."

He winced. He'd not heard her name said aloud for longer than he could remember. Preferred it that way.

"An' ye dinnae be a laddie of nine and ten anamore." Her voice was a little bit softer, filled with compassion he didn't want to acknowledge.

"I was twenty." The words came out fragmented. His chest was tight. Hugh sucked in a breath, then another, but it didn't help.

"Dinnae matter." Aunt Mab's gnarled hand gripped the top of the cane he'd carved for her. Her mouth was set in a determined line, but her eyes were kind when he finally had the guts to meet her gaze. "Ye dinnae be ready ta wed when Brenna MacInnes came to Armadale. Yet ye did yer duty ta yer clan an' ta yer stubborn da."

"An' she died birthing my child, taking the bairn with her."

"God's plan was different from ours. Ye felt Brenna's loss fer a long time. We all did."

"I dinnae love her," Hugh blurted.

Mab grabbed his forearm and squeezed. She laughed, but it wasn't unkind. "Laddie, ye dinnae get tha chance ta love her. She was taken so soon. Brenna was a lass of six an' ten. No more ready fer marriage than ye were."

"She did her duty."

"Aye, as we all do. 'Tis how the world works, my lad."

Emotion choked him, and Hugh forced a nod, because he hadn't cried — well, ever. He wasn't about to start in front of his aunt.

"Yer a good laird, an' a good man. But now ye have one more duty ta see ta."

"I do?"

"Aye, my lad. Ye've a duty ta yerself. An' a duty ta Juliette."

Hugh shook his head.

"Dinnae give me tha' nonsense. Ye love tha' lass. Ye never intended ta, I ken tha' well. It happened, an' she loves ye too. So, swallow yer pride an' hie ta the MacLeods. Get her back. Ferget about the Fae, magic, an' the distant future. Bare yer heart an' wed tha' lass."

chapter twenty-one

Zombieism overtook her as Cormac escorted her into the great hall. Her limbs were heavy, and each step forward made her gut tighter, until every breath crushed her lungs like a vise—oh, and her heart, too.

No. Wait.

Jules didn't have a heart anymore. It was a black hole, burning her from the inside out. She wanted to crumble by the big hearth and give in to her hurt. Sob like she'd never cried before.

He left me.

Rode away like he had lightning up his ass.

"Are ye well, milady?" Cormac's deep voice made her jump. His long blond hair was loose today and shifted around his shoulders. He was one of the few fair-haired MacLeods, and just as big and handsome as the rest of her sister's clan.

She met his dark eyes, so unlike Hugh's, even though they were the same color. "I'm...great."

Liar.

Jules forced a smile.

Cormac didn't believe her, but he didn't call her on it, either. "The ladies are likely in tha solar."

She nodded. "I'll find them." She trudged up the stairwell, not waiting to see if the MacLeod guard was waiting for her.

Jules fought doubling over as pain consumed her. She'd been shot before, but it hadn't hurt as bad as she did right now.

Her hand shook as she opened the closed door to the bright room, locking her knees so she wouldn't fall over.

"Jules!" Claire was alone in the room — thank God. "You're back!" Her sister's smile faded just as it was born. "What's wrong?"

"Nothing."

"Liar."

Jules shook her head and took a seat.

Claire moved away from the fireplace. She'd been rocking a cradle. "He's fussy today; I don't think he feels well." She gestured to her sleeping son. "Just got him down for a nap."

"Where're Alana and Janet?"

Her sister's eyes were full of excitement.

It worked for Jules. Anything to keep the spotlight off her.

"Alana is with Janet. Xander, too, I'd expect. Her back was hurting this morning, so I'm pretty sure it was the start of labor. Who knows, we might have a baby today!"

Jules forced a smile she wasn't feeling. "Oh, awesome."

Claire smiled back and nodded. "It's a boy, like Angus said. He's got magic, but we don't know if he'll be born with wings."

"Wings?"

"Xander has wings, but not in our realm—at least most of the time. Janet sorta…recharges his magic, so he said sometimes his back itches, and once he woke up with his wings. They disappeared again after a few minutes, but who knows, maybe the longer they're together he might get them back. I know he misses flying, even if he's too polite to talk about it."

"Weird."

Her sister smirked. "Right, like that's the only thing weird around here."

"I need to go home," Jules blurted.

Claire squared her shoulders. "What happened?"

"Nothing. Wasn't that always the plan? You're fine. Happy, and all that. I know now that you'll be okay. I can go. I came, I saw. Got kidnapped. Twice. We said goodbye, he dropped me off and…" She shrugged, averting her gaze. Emotion choked her and she refused to cry in front of her sister.

"Jules…"

Jules shook her head and swallowed before she could look at Claire. Forced a smile. Reached for her inner tough cop. It didn't work worth a shit. "I'm good."

"You aren't."

Silence fell, but she couldn't bring herself to

confirm or deny. Her sister knew her too well to buy her bullshit anyways.

"I really should get back. Dan and I were working a murder-suicide when I left, and—"

"Hugh isn't Brent."

Jules fought the urge to crush her eyes shut.

Claire brought up my ex.

Am I that *transparent?*

Jules straightened her back and pressed her shoulders into the back of the chair until the wood bit into her skin. Ignored the breath she should take, but it wouldn't make her head spin any less anyway. She met her sister's green eyes. "God, no. How could he be? Four hundred years is kinda different."

Claire gave her a long look. "You know damn well what I meant, *Juliette.*"

Jules cringed. "Don't call me that."

"Why? Because Hugh does?" Her sister smirked.

She frowned.

Her sister leaned over and squeezed her forearm. "Just...don't go back because you think you *have* to."

"I'm not," she said.

Too quickly if Claire's expression was any indication.

Jules had to get back to her life, didn't she?

Wasn't her partner giving her a hard time for staying in Scotland when he'd said he needed her to come back?

They had cases to work. Bad guys to catch—not

just the *open and shut* they'd been on when she'd had to take off for Scotland. Jules and Dan might not always get along, but they usually managed well enough to work together.

That mattered more than the guy she'd fallen for, didn't it?

Four hundred years in the past.

Her life would be drastically different if she stayed.

No more being a detective.

Jules loved her job. Always had.

Did she love Hugh more?

Yes.

She closed her eyes and sucked in a breath.

Her *everything* hurt.

Claire speaking snagged her attention, and thankfully pulled her out of her head.

"It won't be today, anyway. Alana will be busy if the baby comes, and Angus will have to help open the rift in time. Human blood is necessary, evidently. Full-blooded Fae can't do it."

Great. Let the torture continue.

"That's fine," Jules croaked. "It'll let me spend more time with you and Lachlan. Say a proper goodbye, even." By the end of her statement, her voice had evened out. Someone who didn't know her wouldn't even know something was wrong.

"If I get a vote, I want you to stay." Claire's low remark tugged at her, but the pain didn't fade.

"What if I don't know whose vote should count more...yours or mine? What if the person I want most to vote already let me go? *He* cast...his vote." Jules swallowed the tears that threatened and cursed when Claire's gaze offered concern...and love.

She lost the battle. Her vision clouded and she had to look away from her younger sister. Again.

Claire was up off her chair in two seconds, enfolding her in a warm embrace that just made Jules feel worse.

"I love him," she blurted.

"I know." Her sister's answer was a whisper. No judgment.

Jules crushed her eyes shut against Claire's shoulder and squeezed her tight.

"As much as my husband will cringe about it, I'm okay with it. He saved my baby. He can't be that bad."

Jules pulled back and flashed a watery smile. "No, he's not. He's a good man. A good leader of his clan. He...cares about them."

I just wish he cared about me.

"Surly like my big sister?" Claire grinned and wiped Jules' tears away.

"That's why we worked," she whispered. She forced air into her lungs.

"Go get him."

Jules reared back. "What?"

Claire's green eyes bored into hers. "You're gonna have to go back to Armadale and get him, big sis."

She shook her head. "I-I-I—"

"Did you tell him you love him?"

Jules frowned. "No."

"You said you wanted to go home from the start. He doesn't know you want to stay."

"I don't know if I want to stay." She swallowed because she *did* know. Just couldn't say it.

Not even to Claire.

I can't lose Hugh.

Her sister leaned back, perching her hands on her hips. Her green gaze burned. "Okay, I'll admit it. I'm gonna be selfish here. *I'll* beg you to stay. I don't want to lose you, Jules. I want you to stay. I want my kids to know you. I want to see you regularly. I need my older sister. I won't lie. Life's hard. You go to bed at night sore from working your ass off all day, and you wake up early to do it all over again. There's nothing fun like TV and movies, but there are books. Some interesting ones, too. There's not much time to be bored, anyway. And when you have a big, strong, *hot* husband, the nights are better than any movie, anyway." Claire grinned, chasing some of the somberness in her expression away.

Jules couldn't help but smile. "It's different for me and Hugh than it was for you and Duncan."

"How?"

"Duncan loves you."

"Hugh loves you." Her sister's retort had Jules' stomach flipping, but she shook her head.

"Not that he said. He's still got a thing for his dead wife."

"Bullshit."

She arched a brow at her sister's hard tone and shook her head again. "This is crazy."

Claire laughed and Jules' eyes snapped to her face. "Something funny?"

"Nah. I just thought you'd be beyond the '*this is crazy*' stage. You've been here for a while."

"Well, maybe I've gone nuts then. I went back in time to find my sister and ended up kidnapped. Then I fell in love with my kidnapper. I need a gold medal for Stockholm Syndrome, or just a good shrink. Especially since I'm actually contemplating *staying* here."

"You are? Yay!" Claire clapped. Her face lit up, and she looked so damn pretty.

Jules mock-glared. "You do realize you're *not* helping."

Her sister beamed. "Yup."

"Just leave off, okay, little sister? I don't want to talk about this."

Smile fading, Claire cocked her head to one side, making those long fair locks dance over her shoulder and around her hips. "Not talking about it doesn't change a damn thing."

"No, but it'll make me feel better."

She rolled her eyes. "No, it won't."

"I really don't like you sometimes." Jules stopped short of sticking her tongue out at Claire, like she had done so many times when they were little.

"Comes with the territory. Sisters and all that."

She smirked; she couldn't help herself.

A baby's cry sliced through the air. Lachlan was sitting in the small cradle, his little hand clutching the side as he hollered, tears streaming down his chubby little cheeks.

Saved by the kiddo.

Claire waggled her finger in Jules' face as she whirled away. "We're not done with this."

That's what I'm afraid of.

chapter twenty-two

hugh cringed as his aunt's words refused to stop haunting him. He wanted to stab something.

He growled and nudged Dubh into a canter. His stallion obliged and he leaned down, tempted to close his eyes as chilly air kissed his face.

The wind kicked up her scent that must still be clinging to him, his clothing, and even his damn horse.

At another time, if loss wasn't crushing him, he might've laughed that Juliette had had the guts to steal *his* stallion right out of MacDonald stables when she'd run away. She wasn't a fool. His lass would've known he would come after her.

Come after her, Hugh had. Then walked away.

After Mab's plea, he'd packed a bag and left again, without another word. Hadn't been home since.

Jesus. Has it already been three days?

Hugh had taken Juliette on the beach—no. He'd made love for the first time in his life.

But was it?

Perhaps he'd *made love* every time he'd lain with Juliette. He'd never held a woman so tightly the whole time—let alone afterwards. Overnight. Keeping her in his bed had been *right*.

Now she was gone.

Would Hugh know the moment she went forward in time?

Would he be able to *feel* it somehow?

Or had she already gone?

Dubh slowed to a walk on his own, but Hugh didn't correct his gait.

Misery dominated his mind—and his wretched heart.

He hadn't loved sweet, reserved Brenna. As Mab had mentioned, Hugh hadn't really had the chance. She'd been taken from him.

Now the woman he wanted…the woman who'd stolen his heart…the woman he *did* love had taken *herself* from him.

Hugh's gut roiled.

A part of him wanted to rush Dunvegan's walls, demand they release her. Then again, they weren't holding Juliette against her will.

She was where she *wanted* to be.

The other half of him dreaded it was already too late. It had been three days, after all.

His heart missed a beat and Hugh leaned back, crushing his eyes shut. He held Dubh's reins so tight his knuckles throbbed, but his fingers wouldn't loosen. He sucked in cold air—if he didn't force a breath, his lungs were going to seize, refuse to expand.

The rustling of fabric had his head whipping around.

Hugh stared down the beach, then watched the waves crash into the shore. Other than moving water, he saw nothing.

He glanced down, but the MacDonald plaid under his arse was flat to Dubh's wide back where his body wasn't covering it. The wind had died down, and his stallion was slowly walking over rocks and sand.

No urgency from his mount.

Hugh froze and tugged Dubh to a stop. Narrowing his eyes, he scanned the area before and behind him. The rustling sounded again, and he tilted his head to the side, trying to discern the direction.

He dismounted and drew his claymore.

Something's wrong.

He saw the billowy skirts of the lass running before his eyes took the time to study her frame.

Long dark hair flowed around her form as she ran toward him. She held the fabric high, her ankles and bare feet showing as she ate up the distance between them.

The Irish lass.

Bairn thief.

Hugh tensed and darted away from Dubh. His stallion tossed his head and snorted as if he sensed tension, but he didn't wander as he shifted from hoof to hoof.

Dubh was as restless as he had been the first time, they'd run into the halfling. Perhaps his mount was sensing magic.

The lass saw him and started chanting something in Gaelic, but he couldn't make out more than inflection. Her words went up and down in a cadence he'd never heard the likes of before.

Pain barreled into his stomach and raced up and down his limbs. Hugh cursed and dropped his claymore to the pebbly ground as his grip refused to hold. His fingers burned as if buried in fire and his joints jerked of their own accord.

"Nay!" The shout was ripped from his lips, and he fought the pain, moving to the lass instead of away. Every muscle seared as if flames crept over his body, slowly consuming him from the inside out.

Sweat was born on Hugh's brow and rolled down his temples onto his cheeks. It stung his eyes and made his lips itch, but he couldn't raise his hands to wipe his face.

Still, she ran at him, but he struggled against the agony.

He threw his head back and roared. Hugh panted, chest stabbing at him as he tried to breathe normally.

When their eyes met, an evil smile spread over her full mouth.

She slowed.

Now the lass was only a few feet from him.

Hugh fought the buckle of his knees, straightening his legs, arms, and back with all his might. He hollered again, hoping to God, someone heard him.

Dubh screamed but Hugh couldn't turn to see if

the lass was harming his beloved horse.

"Fall, big man," she commanded. The Fae halfling spread her palms wide, fingers open, and motioned downward.

Hugh's legs refused his order to hold him upright. He gave a final roar as he hit the loamy ground against his will. White-hot pain flared into his knees and thighs.

She laughed, flashing a maniacal grin. The lass increased her chants and started circling his body.

True fear gripped his gut with both hands as pain crippled him. Hugh doubled over.

I am going to die.

Juliette's face flashed through his mind, and he was glad she was already gone. So, she wouldn't— *couldn't*—see this.

The world started spinning, then tilted on its axis when he toppled over.

The lass flipped her palm, and Hugh's body responded as if commanded, splaying him on his back. Pebbles bit at his shoulders and spine. He grunted, but he couldn't move, not even his head. He could only look up at the sky. Twilight was just starting to descend, the moon barely visible.

Another equine scream parted the air and Hugh heard hooves pounding.

Dubh.

Yet another scream sounded—this time a feminine one—then a shouted curse in Irish Gaelic.

Then — *blessedly* — nothing.

Hugh sucked in air as the weight lifted off his chest and he could breathe again. However, he couldn't move.

His stallion snorted and hooves came into his line of sight.

"Dubh," Hugh croaked.

Dubh snorted again, his wide nostrils flaring as Hugh managed to squint up at him. The stallion lowered his great head and nudged his side.

"Give me a minute, lad." Hugh relaxed into the sandy ground and took another breath — then two more, both deeper than the one before it.

His horse pranced backwards as if he sensed Hugh needed some space.

Hugh pushed to his knees. His head reeled but he fought through it and planted his hands into the sand. He was slow to gain his feet — and his bearings.

Dubh shot forward and Hugh threw an arm over his neck, grateful for his horse's assistance in his remaining upright. Once again, it was as if the stallion knew he needed the help.

Hugh scanned the area. The lass lay a few feet away, sprawled on the sand. She appeared to be unconscious — or dead.

Blood pooled on the right side of her head.

He scrambled free of Dubh and stumbled to the lass.

When Hugh prodded her side with a boot, she

didn't respond. He knelt at her side and watched the rise and fall of her chest. He tilted her head to one side. There was a long gash behind her right ear. It was deep and disappeared into her hairline.

So, she'd hit her head on a rock when she'd fallen. Passing out had cut off her chanting, which must've released the magic.

Dubh saved my life.

Hugh swallowed, as his stomach dropped. If he was a lesser man he'd give in to the fear and relief mixing in his gut. He cleared his throat.

He'd known about magic and heard about every Fae legend known to Scotland his whole life. That didn't mean he'd bought into any of it.

Even the day he'd rescued Lachlan MacLeod and this lass had thrown something to the ground to disappear, Hugh had rationalized it could've been a mixture of herbs.

He'd met Alex MacLeod's wife and her cousin and believed them to be Fae. Hell, he'd believed his Juliette from the moment she'd told him she was from the future and magic had brought her to his time.

However, magic had not *impacted* him until today.

When it'd almost stolen his life.

Words.

Words had almost killed him.

Hugh blew out a breath as tremors chased each other down his spine. He glanced up at Dubh when his horse neighed, as if to ask if he was well. "I'm braw, laddie."

The stallion trotted to him, pushing at his shoulder with his soft nose.

He managed a small smile and reached to pat Dubh's neck.

Hugh stood and dug into the pack he'd been smart to grab when he'd left Armadale. He'd intended to stay gone a few days—he'd not wanted to hear another word Mab had to say about Juliette.

He was glad he'd grabbed rope he'd not anticipated needing, and quickly bound the lass' hands and feet.

Running his hands over her body, he felt for a belt-pouch or any pockets. His aunt had always sewn pockets into her garments, saying a woman needed a place to put her secrets.

The lass' skirt had none, but there was a strap of leather around her neck.

He couldn't see what was hanging from it; it was buried in the neckline of her leine. Hugh tugged until it snapped, catching the prize in one hand.

A leather pouch.

"Wha' have we here?" Hugh turned it over, squeezing. Something small and hard was enclosed inside it. He stared at the unconscious lass, but she didn't stir. He needed to work quickly; he had no idea how long she would be out.

He opened the pouch and dumped its contents onto his flat palm. Two crystals gleamed in the fading light, one black and one clear. There was also a piece of gold. Uncut, a nugget that would be worth a great deal, even in its current condition.

"Hmmm...."

The three stones were covered in a dark powdery substance.

Hugh shook the pouch and more dark grains fell to the sand at his feet. He didn't know what it was, but something made a shudder rack his frame.

It felt bad.

Dark.

Evil.

He shoved the crystals and gold back into the pouch, tugging the drawstring tight and knotting it twice—just in case.

Hugh shoved the magic tools into his bag on Dubh's back. He'd no desire to have them near his body, so he didn't want them in the pocket of his trews.

He hefted the lass up, and again tremors threatened moving up his arms and settling in his chest. Hugh really didn't want to touch her. A sense of foreboding hovered, flipping his stomach, but he wouldn't have the lass with him long.

She was destined for justice.

The halfling needed to pay for her crime, even though the lad had come to no harm.

Dubh snorted and tossed his head, darting away when Hugh approached with the lass in his arms.

"Come to me, Dubh." He kept his voice low, using

his most cajoling tone.

The stallion obeyed but danced backwards when Hugh tried to drape the unconscious lass across his wide back.

"I'm sorry. Dinnae be long, I vow ta ye. I find her unbearable as well."

His horse grunted and flared his nostrils, hoofing the rocks. However, he stood still so Hugh could approach again and accomplish his task.

He laid her face down, swinging himself astride his horse and placing a hand on her back so she wouldn't tumble off Dubh.

Even that small touch made his skin crawl.

"Come, laddie. Let's hie ta Dunvegan an' get rid a' this wretch!"

Dubh shot down the beach without a physical command, as if he wholeheartedly agreed.

chapter twenty-three

etting the MacLeods to let him in the gate wasn't a problem this time, despite it being full dark when he'd ridden in. The three oversized guards had taken one look at the Irish lass and stepped aside so he could ride right into the bailey.

Then they closed the outer gates — for the night.

Hugh arched a brow at Cormac MacLeod.

Was he invited to stay the night?

He shrugged. Would be acceptable. Assisted nicely in his quest to avoid his aunt, too. Although him leaving for a day or two was nothing new, Mab would likely think him dead — or at least worry that harm had come to him if he didn't go home on the morrow. He'd planned to go home, telling himself he was done licking his wounds.

Juliette may still be here.

His heart thundered. It mattered not. They'd parted ways three days ago, after the most perfect week and a half of his life.

Again, Mab's voice pounded into his head. *Ye love tha' lass. So, swallow yer pride an' hie ta the MacLeods. Get her back. Ferget about the Fae, magic, an' the distant future. Bare yer heart an' wed tha' lass.*

It had nothing to do with pride, did it?

Hugh was here now, should he not see if she remained?

The pounding of boots sounded, and his eyes darted to the sound—which was accompanied by torches blinking in and out as they came toward him.

Duncan and Alex MacLeod, as well as their father and the Fae man surrounded Hugh and Dubh.

"Why is it I'm always bringin' ye somethin' ye lost?" Hugh tried to tease, but his smirk faded when he saw the murderous expression on Duncan MacLeod's face.

It wasn't aimed at him.

"Ye found tha halfling," the man breathed.

"Aye. She…almost killed me."

Four sets of eyes snapped to his face.

"Your aura is clouded by a dark spell. Come, my cousin can cleanse you." The white-blond man stepped forward, gesturing with the lit torch.

"Ye'd have me inside?" Hugh asked.

"Aye, ye saved my son. Ye brought me tha halfling. I've no ill words fer ye, MacDonald." Duncan met his eyes when Hugh dismounted.

Duncan took the Irish lass from his stallion's back but didn't hold her long. The Fae man took her, holding her high against his chest.

The laird shouted for a lad to take Dubh. "Besides, we've things ta discuss," Alex said.

The Fae man muttered something under his

breath. When Hugh looked at him again, his eyes were closed, and he was chanting words that sounded Gaelic, but were off somehow.

Hugh could make nothing out. Alarm washed over him, and he tensed.

"Relax," Alex MacLeod said. "He's makin' it so she dinnae wake."

"She really almos' killed ye?" Duncan asked.

Hugh forced a nod. Admitting what happened on the beach should've made him feel weak but it didn't.

"Come, I'll have my wife fix ye." The MacLeod laird gestured.

"I'll take her to the dungeon myself, and seal the locks with a spell," the Fae man said. "I shall meet you when I've finished." He disappeared in the darkness of the bailey.

"We'll be in my ledger room," Alex called.

Hugh looked around the vast great hall as he followed the MacLeod twins and their father inside Dunvegan. His heart sped up and he cursed it. He couldn't muster the bollocks to ask about Juliette.

The door was wrenched open, and Jules popped up, her heart running a mile a minute in the borrowed bed. She hadn't been sleeping just yet, but Claire had still startled her. "Jesus! What's wrong?"

One look at her sister told her there was nothing

wrong. Not if the grin she was wearing was any indication. "Hugh's here!"

Her stomach fluttered and she schooled her expression to mask the plummeting feeling seizing her gut. Instinct made Jules want to shout, *'so what?'* but she bit it back. It was bad enough she'd been stuck at Dunvegan for three days. She didn't need to hear his name when she was finally getting somewhere on convincing herself to forget him.

Yeah, that's working.

It wasn't like she could get mad at Janet. The brunette beauty had finally delivered a healthy boy, and she and Xander had named him Liam. The birth had been difficult; everyone was exhausted but okay now.

Jules hadn't had the heart to be a pest begging to get out of Dodge. Seeing the little guy made it worth it, too. Beautiful baby. Dark-haired like his mom, violet eyes like his dad, and no wings after all.

"You scared the shit out of me for that?" Jules barked.

Claire arched one fair eyebrow, resting her hands on her hips. Despite the late hour, her sister was still dressed in the olive-green skirts she seemed to love so much. "Right. Like you don't care."

"I don't." Jules averted her gaze, plucking invisible fuzz off the MacLeod tartan covering her.

The plaid's the wrong color.

Oh, shut the hell up.

"Bull. Shit." Her sister crossed the room, her expression about the sternest Jules had ever seen it.

"Oh, hold on to that expression. You're gonna need it when Lan gets older. Great *mommy* face."

"Juliette."

Jules winced, ignoring her baby sister when Claire climbed on the high bed and plopped down. She relaxed into the pillows behind her, resting her head on the carved wooden headboard.

"You're being ridiculous," her sister accused.

She cast her eyes to the wide ceiling. "I'm not going through this with you again. Let me get some sleep so I can mentally prepare for the journey tomorrow. In case you don't remember, traveling through time is a bitch."

"Hugh. Is. Here." Claire pinned her with a pointed stare.

"I heard you twice the first time."

"It's a sign."

"A sign of what? That he lives on the island?"

"Jules. Please—"

She growled and met Claire's green eyes. "Please, *what?*"

"Hugh brought Bridei to us. He told Duncan that she almost killed him with a spell. Alana says it was a spell meant to break every bone in his body."

"What?" The word was a croak, and Jules shot up in the bed, her pulse pounding in her ears. "Is he okay?" She had to swallow hard—twice.

"You *do* care," Claire breathed.

"Of course, I *care*," Jules snapped. "I love him." She winced at her first-class blurt.

Her sister grabbed her hand and squeezed.

"Is he okay?" popped out of Jules' mouth.

It sounded like a demand, but instead of being annoyed, Claire beamed.

"He's fine. Alana washed the residual magic away with a spell of her own. She said he's not in harm's way. She and Xander bound Bridei's magic and Duncan threw her in the dungeon."

"Dungeon? Like a real one? Y'all have a dungeon?"

Her sister giggled and nodded. "Aye. It's dark and smelly and has bars like jail. Only three cells and I don't venture down there."

"Jesus."

Claire laughed again. "You sound like Duncan. Except, of course, for the sexy brogue."

Jules couldn't hold back her smile. "Yeah, yeah. Hugh says it all the time. Has that sexy brogue thing going on, too."

"Actually, he has sexy going on all over. He's kinda hot, big sis."

"Claire Grace! You're a married woman."

Her sister laughed. "I still have eyes. And I'd never mack on my sister's man even if I wasn't married. Just sayin'."

Jules' smile faded. "He's not my man."

Claire sobered. "Don't lose him just because you're stubborn. Don't go back if you really want to stay."

"Did he ask about me?" When her sister didn't answer, Jules crushed her eyes shut and clenched her jaw until her teeth smarted. "That pretty much says it all right there, Claire-bear."

"No, it doesn't."

When she finally had the guts to meet Claire's eyes, she wanted to cry even more. All she read was concern. Jules couldn't stand it. She needed anger. It was better. Trying to muster it was a failure. "Yes, it really does."

Claire shook her head, and her smile was kind. "He's a Highlander, Jules. Remember that. *Stubborn* is engrained. As strong as he is physically. Not to mention what he's been through. Whether he loved her or not, he lost his wife and child. These men protect what is theirs. Always. He didn't have the control to do so."

"All you're doing is highlighting our differences. Everything definitely in the *con* column." It was Jules' turn to shake her head.

"Love is the only important *pro*."

Jules frowned and swallowed against the lump in her throat. "It would never work. I love my job. I can't do that here. Being a woman is a con in this century."

"Doesn't bother me as much as I thought it would," Claire said softly.

"You have Duncan."

"You have Hugh."

Jules frowned harder, this time at how fast her sister had countered. "I don't."

"You could."

"You're killin' me."

Claire's mouth was a hard line. "I won't apologize. Stop being a dumbass. What do you have to go back to? Need I remind you we have no *family* there? You don't like your partner even if you love your job. You don't like your boss all that much either, and you haven't been in a relationship that mattered since I was a kid. Brent was a dick, and you never should've married him, so he doesn't count. You want to walk away from the man you actually fell in love with just because he wasn't born in the same century you were?"

"Fuck," Jules whispered.

"I totally could be right now, actually. But I'm sitting here with you." Her sister waggled her eyebrows.

Jules laughed. "Claire. Really?"

Claire smirked. "You just hate that I make sense."

"I do."

"Finally. Something that happens to be the truth."

"Bite me."

Her sister flashed a smartass grin, and shook her head, long flaxen locks dancing over her shoulders. "No thanks, not my thing. Look, *he's* here. *You're* here. Why don't you at least talk to him? Tell him how you feel. Find out how *he* feels and if it's not what you want to hear — which has like nil chance of happening — you can still go in the morning."

"I can't." Jules ignored how her heartrate sped up with each of Claire's words.

"You can. You just *won't.* I never knew you to be a runner. That was always my game, not yours. You always faced the giant alone."

Jules closed her eyes again as her sister's observation had sting Claire probably didn't intend. "I never faced the giant alone. You were always there, no matter what shitty foster family we were living with."

"But I hid behind you, clinging to your hand." This was soft and full of regret.

Emotion that had nothing to do with her broken heart rolled over Jules and a tear trailed down her cheek. "You were little. You were supposed to." She forced words out.

Claire threw her arms around her. "You always saved me. Now let *him* save *you.* He loves you, big sister. I just know it. You don't always have to be the strong one."

Her voice evaporated as her sister pulled away. Tears coursed down and Jules couldn't even make her hand move so she could wipe them away.

"Just think about what I said. Oh, and down the hall, toward the stairs. Third door on the right." Claire hopped off the bed, grin back in place.

"Wh-h-hat?" Jules cleared her throat.

"Hugh's room."

Her sister was gone before she could shout, "So what?"

CHAPTER TWENTY-FOUR

"What the hell am I doing?" She winced at the disgust in her tone as she paced the corridor.

Claire would have a freaking field day if she knew where Jules was.

Thanks for the tip, lil' sis.

Not even two minutes had passed after Claire had left her guestroom before Jules had shoved her legs into pants and her arms into a shirt and hurried to the room Hugh had been shown to.

Can you spell pathetic?

Yeah.

It's five letters and starts with a J.

Her heart rebounded against her ribs, making fun of her as it went for the lay-up. It was bouncing around so much it might as well kick her in the gut on the way, too. Her mouth was a desert with no hope of an oasis.

If Jules ever got the balls to form a fist and knock, it wouldn't matter. She wouldn't be able to speak to him.

Stop playing coward.

She sucked in a breath that only made her throat ache even more and forced a knock on the door.

Jules waited…and waited.

She resisted the urge to glue herself to the rough wood and beg him to open up. Emotion swallowed her whole and made her shake so bad even her teeth rattled.

He's not coming.

Somehow, he knew it was her and didn't want anything to do with her.

When the door finally opened, Jules had to bite her bottom lip to keep from crying out. She blinked to clear her vision, cursing her tears to hell and back.

His dark eyes widened, and she tried not to fidget as he trailed her frame. "Juliette," Hugh breathed.

"Hi," she blurted.

Idiot.

Jules tried not to stare, but he'd answered her knock wearing only what he called *short pants* — closest thing to boxers seventeenth century style, except they were longer, stopping just above the knee. They hugged his muscular thighs. His calves were bare, and she couldn't help but remember them entwined on that MacDonald blanket on the beach.

The other morning felt like a lifetime ago — in a bad way.

Hugh's gorgeous chest was on display, and she averted her gaze from his pecs — and banished the memory of his hardness against her softness.

Everything Jules was screamed for him. To touch him. Kiss him. Be in his arms again.

"I dinnae think ye'd be here."

The rawness of Hugh's voice had her eyes flying back to his face.

She swallowed a whimper.

His expression matched his tone, suggesting he gave a damn.

"Are you okay?" Jules' second blurt of the night had confusion darting across his face.

"Aye. Why dinnae?"

"Uh…Claire told me about the spell—"

"Oh." Hugh gestured with his hand. "I'm braw."

"Good."

I'm not.

They stared at each other, and Jules shifted on her bare feet. She'd been in a hurry to leave her room, and the cold stone beneath her was only obvious now.

Hugh's eyes darted down before meeting her gaze again. "Come in, lass." He stepped back and put his hand out.

Jules only hesitated for a second, but she couldn't look at him. She avoided glancing at the large bed too, but she didn't miss that the covers were turned back.

Great. He'd been sleeping.

She whirled around to see him hovering near the closed door. "I'm sorry I woke you."

Hugh stepped forward, his arms at his sides. "Ye dinnae."

"Oh. Good." Jules rubbed her arm, but the linen of the leine felt rough and uncomfortable. "What are they going to do with Bree?" She rushed her words, still unable to meet his eyes. Claire hadn't said, and she wanted to know, even if she was currently just trying to divert attention from herself.

"Turn her over ta tha Fae."

"Really? Wow. What will they do to her?"

Her barbarian closed the distance between them, reaching for her hand.

Jules couldn't find it within herself to pull away. A jolt of electricity shot up into her shoulder when their skin met, and she almost lost it.

Or worse—gave in to the urge to let blurt number three out of her mouth. It played on the tip of her tongue and went something like *I love you.*

"I dinnae ken. But dinnae be fer ye ta concern yerself abou'." Hugh's words were low and not condescending in the least. In his way, he was trying to protect her from horrific things.

The Jules-not-in-love-with-him would have been pissed off. She was not *that* Jules. Not anymore, but a part of her couldn't let it go, and she gave in to the urge to defend herself. "I'm a cop, Hugh. Remember when I told you about my job? Investigations? I've pretty much seen it all."

Was a cop.

Was she really willing to walk away from it?

Jules hadn't made a decision before she'd left her room—had she?

Did it even matter?

She hadn't told him how she felt about him.

What if he didn't care?

What if he doesn't love me back?

Claire had accused her of running away. If Hugh MacDonald crushed her heart, she would *need* to run.

"I remember. Dinnae mean ye need ta dwell."

The second defense she'd mustered melted away when Jules met those dark eyes.

Hugh wasn't demeaning her. He was…showing her he cared?

"I am glad yer here, lass." His voice dropped even more, and he reached to tuck one of her messy waves behind her ear.

"I'm glad you're here, too." Tears welled and Jules tried to look away but couldn't. Her heart skipped when Hugh smiled.

She was enveloped in his heat when he tugged her into his arms. Jules wrapped her own around him and squeezed until a low chuckle reached her ears, as well as rumbled against her breasts.

"I need ta breathe, lass."

Jules smiled against his shoulder and closed her eyes. She couldn't speak, even though her heart demanded she tell him she loved him. Her tongue was swollen, stuck to the roof of her mouth.

Hugh rubbed her back in long soothing circles and she melted into him, lulled. Had they not been standing; she could've fallen asleep. Where she belonged. In his arms.

"I failed ye, lass."

His words had her whipping her head up.

Their gazes collided.

"What? How?"

Emotions that made Jules' heart trip danced across his face and shone from his eyes. Tenderness and heat. Then more — something she couldn't bear to put a word to, in case she was wrong.

"I dinnae ask ye ta stay wit' me."

"Did you want to?"

"Aye."

Silence fell and they stared at each other.

Jules felt everything. *Every* part of his body against hers. Chest to breasts, hips to hips, even their legs where they touched. His heart, his breathing was completely in tune with hers.

She couldn't walk away from him.

Rightness washed over her.

"Mab says I failed myself, too."

His mouth was a hard line and Jules wanted to kiss the look off his face.

Then she wanted to take his hand, drag him to that big bed, and beg him to take her.

"In that case, I failed you just as much," she whispered.

Hugh stilled. He said nothing, but his dark gaze bored into her.

Down to her very soul.

Her body warmed from that look, as much as his

strong arms around her. Jules' breath caught and she made herself return that intensity as she threw caution to the wind. "I love you."

Hugh's lips parted. Air rushed out, kissing her face like she wanted to kiss him. His Adam's apple bobbed, but not once did he even try to look away.

Heat crept up her neck when he continued to stare in silence.

Jules didn't know whether to laugh or cry.

She couldn't retreat, and it was a damn good thing he was holding her up. She would be on her ass at his feet otherwise.

Waiting for the pain, the devastation that was about to hit, she wanted to close her eyes. However, she didn't like the coward game she'd been playing, so she didn't.

Jules just stared and waited for Hugh to rip her heart in half...or more likely, a million pieces.

"Juliette..." His chest heaved against her as he took a deep breath. "I love ye, lass." He threw his head back and laughed. "I love ye more than my own life."

Jules blinked.

What did he just say?

Hugh said it a few more times before it computed.

"Dinnae cry, lass. My lass. My Juliette, *mò bhilis*." He cupped her face and thumbed away tears she hadn't known were there.

Hugh loved her?

He loves me.

He. Loves. Me.

Jules froze, waiting to wake from what had to be a cruel dream.

The man she loved smiled, and her stomach somersaulted. Then his mouth descended and took hers, the way he'd taken her heart, pushy, raw, and completely Hugh MacDonald.

She whimpered and snaked her arms around his neck. "I love you." Jules pressed the words into their kiss. "I love you." Then she got down to the business of kissing her man.

Hugh pulled his lass closer, deepening their kiss. Emotion washed over him, and for the first time it wasn't some sort of anger.

Love.

He was full of love and wasn't ashamed in the least.

Juliette loved him.

She whimpered and tightened her grip around his neck as their tongues tangled, both of them pushing mutual desperation into their fused mouths.

His cock ached, and he grunted when she pitched her hips into his. Rubbing against him. His lass had too many clothes on.

Hugh wanted to rip her trews down, tear her leine off and shove her into the borrowed bed behind him, but things were not settled between them. He needed to be clear about what he wanted.

He wanted Juliette.

Forever.

It took more willpower than he knew he possessed to pull away from her kiss. "Lass," he breathed.

Her gorgeous breasts rose and fell against him as Juliette panted and his heart jumped when he met her hazy green eyes.

"Hugh," she whispered.

"Lass. My foundling. My Juliette. Mine."

She smiled.

It was sweet and sensual and tied him in knots.

"I want to be yours."

"Ye are, lass. And I am yers."

Tears welled and spilled again.

Hugh cupped her face and brushed his lips against hers.

"I'm scared, Hugh." Her voice was so low he'd almost missed it, but her words stilled his heart.

"A' what, *mò bhilis?*"

Juliette paused at his endearment, but he didn't tell her what it meant.

She was more than his sweet, anyway. She was his love.

His *everything.*

"Staying. Going. I'm petrified. I…want you. That's all I know. I want *you.* I don't know what to do."

Hugh caressed her high cheekbones with his

thumbs. His gut clenched. "I want ye, lass. My Juliette. 'Tis all tha' matters ta me."

She closed her eyes and leaned up to press her mouth to his.

Hugh kept the kiss short—too short for the likes of his body. His cock demanded freedom from his britches as much as it commanded, he slide into Juliette's sweet heat.

He'd never been a man of clever words.

He reached for what he wanted to say, waiting for Juliette to meet his gaze again. "If ye should wan' to stay, an' ye would have me, I'd like us ta wed."

She smiled through her tears. "You're not demanding it?"

"Some things change a man," he murmured.

"What things, Hugh?"

"Ye, lass."

She made a noise and threw herself even tighter against his chest.

Hugh caught her up and kissed her when Juliette wrapped her legs around his waist. His lass kissed him until he couldn't breathe, and until his erection threatened to blow its top in his short pants.

"Lass, I need ye. Now," he groaned into her mouth. He tightened his hold around her and turned toward the huge bed. He burned for her.

"I'll stay. I'll marry you."

Her words had him freezing with her in his arms. Before he'd taken more than a few steps. "Aye?" Hugh breathed.

"Aye." Juliette smiled. "It won't be perfect all the time. We'll clash. But I love you, Hugh. If I went back to the future, I'd regret it for the rest of my life. And If I go back, I can't change my mind. There'd be no one to bring me back to you."

All he heard was *Aye* and *I love you, Hugh.* The rest of her statement didn't penetrate his foggy brain.

"Hugh? Did you hear what I said?"

"Aye," he croaked. "We'll marry on the morrow."

She smirked. "There's my demanding barbarian."

Hugh grinned. "I love ye, Juliette. An' yer wrong, *mò bhilis.*"

"Wrong?" Juliette reared back; a fair eyebrow arched.

"Everything 'twill be perfect."

Juliette grinned and kissed him in answer.

the end

about the author

USA Today Bestselling, award winning author of romantic suspense, epic and historical fantasy romance, C.A. loves to dabble in different genres. If it's a good story, she'll write it, no matter where it seems to fit!

She's a hopeless romantic and always will be. Risking it all for Happily Ever After is what she lives by!

C.A. is originally from Ohio, but got to Texas as soon as she could. She's happily married and has a bachelor's degree in Criminal Justice.

She's always writing, and helps small business owners by writing their websites, and she loves it!

WEBSITE: http://www.caszarek.com
EBOOK STORE:
https://www.caszarek.com/ebook-store
PAPERBACK STORE:
https://www.caszarek.com/paperback-store
FACEBOOK:
http://www.facebook.com/caszarek
INSTAGRAM:
https://www.instagram.com/caszarek/
TWITTER: https://twitter.com/caszarek
BOOKBUB:
https://www.bookbub.com/profile/c-a-szarek
GOODREADS:
https://www.goodreads.com/author/show/5815085.
C_A_Szarek
EMAIL: ca@caszarek.com

You can sign up for C.A.'s newsletter on her website, as well as buy all her books!